MAL

To Ray
with best wishes
Vic Vincent

MAL

An Odyssey of Non-sequential Segments of a Life

by

Vic Vincent

Strategic Book Publishing and Rights Co.

Strategic Book Publishing and Rights Co., LLC
USA | Singapore
www.sbpra.com

For information about special discounts for bulk purchases, please contact Strategic Book Publishing and Rights Co. Special Sales, at bookorder@sbpra.net.

ISBN: 978-1-68181-200-7

Disclaimer

This is a work of fiction. Names, places, characters, and incidents are either a product of the author's imagination or used fictitiously, and any resemblance to actual persons, living or dead, business establishments, events, or locales, is purely coincidental.

Thanks JG

Wherein the observer is the observed?
Just after The Wall Street Crash there was life,
But in Dublin's fair city, where the girls
are so . . .?
Woe to be an issue
Of misshapen tissue
And in the beginning ...
And even then, no one listened to his unheard
screams.

I don't want to go. Please. I don't want to go. Leave me where I am. I want to stay here. Why are you doing all this heaving and convulsing, just to get rid of me? Why are you doing this?

You are my mother of the entire world. Please stop all this straining.

Another great heave and it's into the slippery slope. He was going out, going out from an embryo home, where he had been so safe. You've definitely made your mind up and if you don't stop, I will have to face the world.

They are all so happy among the bright new light. I feel all those hands, as I touch human flesh for the first time, and I will know its closeness forever.

They are all so delighted with their work, as those first earthly sounds are issued, while still within the confines of your limbs. And you, the fruitful mother, are so happy to be disgorged.

The First Hurt

You could say that it was a first earthly sadness when they cut my last line of such intimate communication with you and we would never be so close again. You've suffered all that stretching and tearing, just to let them take your other heartbeat away. Who could predict what the future would hold. Why must we relive memories that can still hurt?

So secure in a cot, when you gave me a maternal slap for the first time and I was shocked. In one moment of a mother's frustration, you shattered a maternal closeness on the occasion of my first involuntary defecation. I was looking in mild curiosity at the object which had issued from my yet, not wholly controlled body, when the admonishing slap was struck on an unsuspecting backside. Why should we be responsible for something which decides to detach itself from us when too young to stop it performing its natural function which nature dictates? Must it only activate, when receptacles are put under, to work like a machine from practically day one, never to malfunction?

Was it mental disintegration at the ripe old age of one? The seeds sown, a vulnerability that would forever endure. Shattered was the impregnable bastion of a mother who could inflict hurt and pain.

He who was the cause of my arrival upon this mortal coil, never bothered to cultivate his imperfect product after issue and, hence a dearth of the love and bonding, so essential in the early stages, was never achieved.

A father's pollen often suffers in transit. Such are the voids which exist between a sire and son, who are so conditioned by a simple act of procreation, which can make such strangers of us all.

Why do we vainly search for the last piece? Is there a piece that could hold the key? Somehow we know there will never be a magical key, but we shall never stop searching and yearning for the answer to the mystery.

In horizontal mode, we seem to attain a higher level of thought processing of such matters. Does the brain work better in the prone position, because it suffers less gravitational pull? Is it so much easier for oxygen to circulate? Is it? All we need is someone to turn the key and unravel it all.

A Motherly Landscape

When a mother's back was turned, like a tiny speck, we crawled up the fleshy white precipice. Such a large area to be traversed, going uphill, uphill, always uphill, counting the notches on the spinal column as steps to be negotiated with great difficulty to climb to her summit.

Tiny hands, clamber over the steps of vertebrae. Come on, heave yourself up with one chubby leg and then another.

To be carrying this weighty napkin, with such a big pin, holding everything in. Were we not climbing to the sky? Another leg heaved up, another step, ascending so slowly, dragging the enormous weight of several pounds, eventually to reach the top.

Always that summit to be reached, and then over so-soft white shoulders, like a snow capped mount, hoping, just hoping, to see the warmth and love of a smile.

She was so young then, with a beautiful face in a time-worn motherly sleep.

A grubby hand thrust through her hair. You were oh so pretty, dearest mother.

Hungering for your love, when you only had to smile and hug, and, when you did, you made the world a heaven on earth. A displeased look from you and the world crashed around a baby's cosmos. But if only you would awaken and give that re-assuring hug of a motherliness glowing.

Of course you didn't know, as you slept in your own private dream, while cherubs climbed and then descended to uncharted depths among your limbs in the warm bedclothes.

Can't see anything now under those blanketing masses around your legs and knees and toes. At the end of the long journey turn around, turn back, and sleep among the secure confines of motherliness.

Then once more, we're crawling around your toes, tripping off such heights, the bedclothes not holding as we slip off the end of the precipice. *Plonk!* And it's all the way to the floor with a bump to awaken and bring a helping hand. What heights to have fallen, having climbed to the sky, and then the light caress and holding hands, as we are drawn so close. The succouring hand always needed, when falling off, and it's just that falling off, always falling, and all the time, always falling. Could someone freeze those seconds of momentary panic?

Who will ever explain such total dependence?

In a later time, it was our father who betrayed her and cleaved to another much younger face, surrendering to a simple soul's unwise infatuation. He had forgotten his first true love, a devoted mother, who had borne him the produce from his seed, who would never understand why he could leave her.

When he had left, to savour his stolen lustful moment, he had broken her heart and her life. Deep down, the scar would never heal.

It was then that she needed a soul to take the place of the void now existing in her bed.

She needed someone there, and a baby did remind her of the love she once had, when he caused me to be conceived.

As time sped along, she could never forget the hurt. She was grieving so when she turned her back and bade me go to sleep without a kiss or cuddle, because of the pain inside her broken heart.

But even so, in those early formative years, dear mother, you had allowed those unforgettable heavenly moments, when you held your child in a new way, which exploded a young and, as yet, undiscovered soul. You said it was all part of growing up and must be forever our lifelong secret, which we would take to our graves. It was the first torment of an innocent love, which was later to be spurned.

A bond of fusion In fleshly union
So cravenly craved And illicitly made.

Is that where it all began, or starts, or ends? We have to get up, lots to do. "Daydreaming over?" He will say it every day, but has he really made his mind up to go and see her. Have we raced too far ahead? In analysis, to expend is self-destructive. It can build up one thing and let down another. To blossom is eventually to fade.

Stop these unproductive ramblings. You said you were going to see her. You've been promising, promising. Oh, queen of queens. When will I see you? May I worship you again? When? When? Oh, when?

Just wait, wait for the next command. Then, once again, you may reach the summit in the land of queenly conquest.

Forward to that regal seam of silk and curve, which is the key to the very life and death of the aspirant? She was always the mother of discharging, or discarding the plaything after exacting the price of procreation.

She was created to be so adept at deploying the tools of the propagation rite, which could destroy feeling and pleasure in an unloving biological exercise. She never gave a thought about the object being used, or abused, in her procreative ritual. Never contemplate the reason, or the human race would die. Oh, Miss Queenly Croft, you made me live to die. Lying here, why do I think of it all? Why don't you get up? Come on, get up, you've things to do. You said you were going to see her.

In a world of make believe, the most personal thoughts must never be expressed audibly or they would lose their special significance in their stolen secrecy. There may be various queens in a life, but there will always be only one who was truly adored and enslaved you in a consuming love, which will always be remembered in its crushing intimacy and hurt, influencing all which came long after.

Just to lie at her feet and await her command. Servility may bring many favours and delights.

The thoughts which clog up one's mind and refuse to go away seem to have a purpose at the time, or to mirror something else, like your deepest thoughts when you so wanted to be with her and didn't, although you said you were going but you didn't. Are you really ever going to see her again? Why do you keep punishing yourself with the very thought of it? Like, you said you were going to see her yesterday, and you did not? Answer please.

When it's all years later and you think back, you knew that involvement with that queen would be destructive. But you craved her so madly, always knowing in the back of your mind it could only have a bad ending. It is the very nature of Queens that, when they have their fill, you are no longer required. We should know that it's nothing personal. It's the natural order. So that was it, was it not? Why do you want to be free from all blame? Is it always going to be, "just blame it on her"? But why should you have a get-out excuse for your stupid actions? Who do you think you are?

Uncle Toby

Why do very early trips to the seaside come to mind in a childhood-clouded memory? It was always Uncle Toby who would decide. As a mere child, I wasn't ever consulted.

It all had to do with his very old car. When I would see him giving it a cleaning, I'd know what was coming.

He'd say to the Mother, "It's such a nice day, I thought to take young Mal to the seaside. He's up in that room too much. The fresh air will do him good."

There would be a nod as she gave a wistful smile of assent. Auntie Geraldine, another dear soul, once had a dream in the shape of Uncle Toby, never to be fulfilled. But she would always cherish him in her own catholic way, because of the vows they had once made.

When they met, he was the knight on the white charger who had a responsible job in the civil service. He was in charge of the post-room. His white charger came in the shape of him mounted on an old Raleigh bicycle, although he graded up to a battered old Ford later on.

When the doctors told Auntie Gerry that she could never have children, Uncle Toby had to conceal a great disappointment. From that time, they seemed to mutually accept that their bodies had no further procreative function, and she could never warm to Uncle Toby again. She knew he understood that in her deep religious beliefs, bodily fusion should only be for one purpose, to bear the fruit of a religious union, as the scriptures had taught her. To do it for pleasure would be a mortal sin and would damn her soul.

And so it was, that he would take me to travel through the environs of the Wicklow and Dublin roads to the seaside, when we would eventually arrive at the gravelly beach at Bray.

While watching the waves, it would not be long before Josie appeared. She was the consolation prize in Toby's life and always seemed to emerge from nowhere. She was much younger than Aunt Gerry and had not as yet suffered the disappointments that inevitably occur in a life.

As if the meeting were totally unexpected, he'd say," Why, if it's not yourself down here again, Miss Josie?"

Then he would take off my clothes and on with the bathing trunks, then into the water's edge. A rubber tube would be put around my middle. He'd exhort in a kind of gentle and coaxing voice, "Young Mal, you paddle and play with the waves for a while and make a sand castle until we get back, when I'll bring you something really special."

A child left on his own, playing in the water's edge, sits on the sand and looks around, wondering with a child's mind where Uncle Toby has gone. Of course, he always returned. In all the times we went to the seaside, he never put on a bathing costume. He would merely roll up his trouser legs and hold me with the tube forever affixed. Having put me afloat he'd say, "Now every time the wave washes you in, paddle out again and that way you'll gain confidence." And then, "We'll be back soon. We're going for a walk. "And then he would add, "I'll bring you back something nice."

Waiting, waiting for him to return could be so lonely.

In the distance I observed a family all bathing so happily. Two lovely children, a father and a mother. Such frolicking, such loving, all belonging to each other. As I watched the little boy, I wished I could have been him. I could have been there in his place. My father could have been holding *me* aloft and splashing *me* and giving *me* a cuddle and then passing me on to my mother who frolicked so lovingly with me. My sister could be that other little girl. Just thinking about it, I was transported.

Oh to be that little boy with that father, mother, and sister, and joy abounding amid the lovely surf. So much joy they didn't know I was sharing.

I lived their lives, as I watched from afar. They might never know I existed, as I savoured every moment through such loneliness, even though I was not being hugged by the proud doting father or caressed by a loving mother, and my sister wasn't splashing me, feigning jealousy. But I wanted it to go on forever, watch them forever, never to stop.

But truly deep down, I never got over the feeling of isolation while waiting for Uncle Toby to return. It was the price, even then, to be exacted.

My uncle's voice broke in on my reverie. He looked a bit dishevelled, but he was smiling. He did bring me a large ice cream. We both knew it was an unashamed bribe. Josie never seemed to return with him after their walk.

"Did you make all those sand castles yourself? Aren't you clever? Don't tell your mother that I left you on your own."

His little deceits gave me happy memories of the seaside and of a generosity with bribes from such an early age.

When he wouldn't be seeing Josie, when he was supposedly on sick leave, he'd do some work for the post office. When I thought about the amount of time he avoided for one reason or another to be at work, considering his amount of "non-input," they seemed to continue to pay him. I often have thought about him since. All those ice creams and sticky buns and the oft repeated, "Don't say I left you on your own, or that I met anyone."

"Yes, Uncle Toby."

He'd give me a hug and a squeeze accompanied by a knowing wink, and I could have forgiven the old rascal anything.

When I was somewhat older, I realised why he should not have had another lady in his life at all. And perhaps Aunt Gerry accepted that a man's need must be. She was not completely deceived.

Eventually, when the Post Office (The Civil Service) and Toby parted, Aunt Gerry had only commented that she wasn't a bit surprised. Apparently, some misdemeanour had been committed that even their most tolerant view could no longer accept.

When the war broke out, he was just one of so many others from the green fields of an Emerald Isle, with no prospect for anything but hard times. So it was that, with many thousands of his brothers, he was off to fight The Hun in foreign lands, as of yore. No one ever heard from Uncle Toby after that. When I mentioned his name, as a child might, the two women just hugged each other.

Aunt Gerry whispered through her tears, "He probably lies like many others, under a marker somewhere. I will always say a prayer for the repose of his soul."

A somewhat older Josie, no doubt, is out there somewhere, who remembers their most intimate stolen moments. A tear would come to her eye as she also remembered a soldier's farewell, when he told her not to cry, as he would be back as soon as John Bull had taught the Hun a lesson. She had waved through the tears as the train pulled out on its way to the North to join the same army as so many of his kind in times present and past. And much later, when, in a freezing wet cold trench, he would be warmed by the memory of the same stolen moments.

The chances were that he would be felled like his comrades in due course, when enemy guns spat their sheets of lead from machine gun nests.

Schooling

Being at school was always associated with feeling pain it seems, because, when you broke their rules, the cane or leather would appear for things like not being able to get there at the proper time or cope with the sums. No matter how hard I tried, I never could give the correct answers.

Corporal punishment was so high on their curriculum. In the beginning, I mostly got the cane because of younger brother Eamonn, who couldn't keep up when we walked all the way to Terenure across wet fields on wintry mornings. It was too far for his little legs.

Sometimes I'd take him pick-a-back, but he was getting so big and becoming such a weight that I would soon tire.

Eamonn's teacher was the kind of mother everyone would love. Miss Duffy was such an angel in charge of her brood, all of such tender years that they were not much more than babes for whom she really cared.

When I brought younger brother to her to be put into her charge for the first time, she had looked at him with love and pity.

She knew it was hopeless. There were too many things which she couldn't change. She took his little hand and led him away to join the rest of her flock.

Even at his tender age, he coughed a lot. He seemed to always have cold wet feet from walking through too many wintry wet fields. He badly needed special nourishment for his tiny frame. Tuberculosis seemed to walk hand in hand, in our pleasant land.

One of the happiest moments that stands out in a far distant time was when Miss Duffy had me sit on her lap. I was the envy of all in our small class. It was pure bliss, to be loved and wanted, even if only for that brief moment, leaving an indelible print that stays forever. She was the first succouring queen in a child's world.

On the opposite side of the spectrum, when a little older, was the stentorian voice of the black-cassocked Christian Brother along the corridor. He would shape our souls for all time in censorious voice, "Hurry along, boy. You're late. Don't dawdle."

I'd have to stand in line again to receive the benefit of corrective measures in the pursuance of making us better Christians.

He wore the black smock with a deep pocket, wherein lay the strap—his instrument which knew how to teach with penal exaction if you didn't get it right. They could never know the pain felt by a young child's cold hands in winter that seemed to hurt forever.

Cecil

There were happy times when I was in charge of Cecil, our main choice of transport, who had four strong legs. He became such an affectionate part of my early formative years. Probably the most willing beast anyone could have. Having said that, he did have a character all his own and occasionally would just have to let you know about it. Perhaps it was the fact that this not-so-ancient mariner of the fields felt he was being put upon. I don't think, looking back, that he liked carrying four small children, all at one time, like when I would invite all and sundry to be my passengers, which of course was not being fair to the noble beast.

I'm remembering Cecil, our magnificent Clydesdale. He could be stubborn, like when he'd choose to stop for no apparent reason. Apart from the delays caused, this wouldn't have been too bothersome, except for the fact that it was invariably when we were crossing water, like in the middle of a stream. He would stop and start his blackmailing bit, with all passengers aboard.

Not until he received his pay-off in the shape of a piece of sugar or juicy carrot or even a small apple would he move forward. I always made sure I had something as a treat to give him. Then, when in receipt, we would move on again. It was his little game, and I had to go along with it. I had no choice. God knows if you didn't have a lump of sugar or carrot, how long this might have gone on. I always forgave him his little proclivities. He knew I loved him and I'm sure he loved me, in his own way.

In between times, Cecil was fully employed doing the heavy work in the fields. That was the penalty for being so big and strong and of a very kindly nature. I often thought afterwards that he was never fully appreciated and had the forbearance of a saint.

Whenever I think of Cecil, I cast my mind back to the smell of wet soil and growing food, most of which was shipped to feed those in far-away lands engaged in world conflict.

Toiling in the Good Earth

We were so young to be stooped low over the long furrows where we sifted the ploughed earth and picked the potatoes or removed the weeds. Each struggling tiny weed was to be dealt with, uprooted and given no chance to grow. The length of the furrows seemed endless. As I worked my way through them, I'd be glad when the cooling breeze eased the ache and the pressure on a very young malformed back, ill-designed for the strained posture.

Everything was so carefully tended so that the tuberous bulb with the green stalks would flourish. The root required to be tended, never to count the cost of toil or tissue expended.

It had formed the staple diet of a land that nourished a people who toiled in what was sometimes unforgiving stony soil for the wherewithal to survive. When it failed in 1845, it had decimated a population and had spread the starving survivors far and wide throughout the new worlds where they had made their mark, and their achievements formed a legacy that will forever be.

The memory of the disaster is still seared so indelibly on the minds of those and their descendants who will never forget. Memories of loved ones long gone, who died from hunger by the roadside.

It was understood and expected that those still at school would tend to the crop in the summer months during holidays and the long summer evenings. We had all been well schooled in the Christian ethic of hard work.

The voice of our kindly pastor: "You mustn't be idle boy. The devil finds work to do for idle hands. Keep your mind and body occupied with healthy and honest toil. Go to it."

That was the maxim on which they based their entire philosophy. So you got the idea that if you shirked, you'd be in trouble. If you don't work, you do not sit at the table.

So many of those at my tender age were obliged to serve their childhood in the same fields as our fathers before, which stole away those precious years when children should have been at play. The only solace one could gain from it was that it was a release from their strictures of classroom, cane or leather strap, and even our home. In the summer when it was warm and the sun shone, it was not so bad, and young souls could even find themselves at play while at toil.

We had winters that could hurt. I always seemed to have cold feet and hand's that never got warm. Was I ever of the least importance in the chain which makes it all work? My executive pay for my labours will be one shilling per furrow which seems to run to the end of the world. They virtually go over the horizon. Will I get to the end today? I move through the corrugated earth at a slow meticulous pace, so that not one weed is missed. When one is less than forty inches high and stands in a furrow more than half that again, with the green stalks on top, the field of view is somewhat restricted. It certainly takes on enormous proportions. Arriving at the end of the long drill could be likened to Scott's arrival at the Pole in a child's mind. And when you got there, you are twelve pence in credit.

This could represent at least a whole day of constant backbreaking endeavour and discomfort.

The longest journey which sticks in my memory was the never-ending length of those drills in the furrowed fields. It was all part of making one's contribution from an early age. On one occasion I nearly got through two in a day, starting at daylight until the dark of the evening. Then the loving hand which took the money away. They'd take care of it and you'd be offered a treat in the form of a "piece" in exchange. You'd be allowed to stay up a little later than usual before being put away into that place of sleep. What prizes and privileges?

They called it the good earth. To live so close to it for so long and have it run through young grubby fingers, then let it drop for no other reason than that you've absorbed the different textures which you can smell as you move through the contouring landscape.

Without standing up to look, you could tell at which point you were.

Those subtle differences of the soil's texture, scent and aroma could tell you everything. Each part of the furrow had its own message for you.

And what about when the heavy summery showers came and the vapour haze arose from the green blooms when the sun reappeared cast its life-giving rays? It spoke a language all its own. The close proximity of this earth you've come to know. It gives and gives and all it asked was that we tend it with love and, given a fair wind, it will feed and save us.

Big Jim

Big Jim, my school friend, could make me wild, but I liked him a lot. We were very friendly when it suited our purpose, like when we were breaking "their" rules. If either could ever gain an advantage, then our friendship would be suspended until hostilities ceased. Mostly, it was when we fought over Sarah. Big J would tell all and sundry that she was his girl, and I used to tell them that she preferred me. Sarah liked the competition which took place for her innocent favours. She secretly enjoyed being competed for at such a tender age. I earnestly hoped that she preferred me. After all, I thought, she had not given Big J a piece of her cake when he'd got the cane. That favour had been reserved solely for me. When I'd taunt him with it, he'd get so jealous. He would tell me that he was her real protector.

Big J, Ginger to you, was a much bigger lad than I in every sense and very strong for his years. He never seemed to stop chewing something. Sometimes I'd thump him in fury and run like hell.

He was built for strength and not for speed. When he could no longer keep up the chase I'd taunt him some more. I gave him a black eye on one occasion, but he made me pay for that by falling on top of me 'til I was near suffocated. He had a nasty way of coming up behind people and giving them a hard slap on the back as in good fellowship. It used to wind me as it did others who would watch him nervously when in their wake. He had made me one of his favourite recipients of this particular treatment, and my only chance of retribution was getting the odd sly punch at him and then run.

On one famous occasion, he sidled up to me and asked me to look at what he'd found. When I looked down at the object of curiosity, it was his own, very private, flowering manhood, of which he was justly proud. It seemed to be maturing at a rapid rate. I was supposed to think that it was funny. When he showed it to me the first time, it made me laugh. Now he was just being boastful and proud of its proportions. This new engorging, swelling toy he had discovered only made me jealous. It seemed to have suddenly come into his possession and I was envious, because I didn't have one like it.

A few months ago it would seem, Big J didn't have any toys to play with, and now nature had given him the greatest of all, and it was continuing to burgeon forth in so many ways. I thought it very unfair at the time.

If he sidled up to me just once more to make me jealous, I swore to myself that I'd do it a mischief.

Then later, as the weeks went by, he showed me how he could make it very large on demand, as he pulled it through his torn trouser pocket. I was now more envious than ever, make no mistake. Its proportions seemed to get larger daily as he allowed me to have a peek. He was at an age when his birth right was coming into full flower. I couldn't look at it for size and was getting more irritated. Why didn't I have one of that dimension too? What made matters worse was the fact that, given the slightest excuse, he was always ready to show it. All you needed to say was, "Let's have a peep, Big J," and, quick as a flash, he'd put his hand into his torn pocket and, *presto*, he'd pull it through for all to see.

Being of a devious nature, even at that tender age, I resolved to play a rather harsh practical joke on him. I don't think I realised the implications at the time. The basis of my plan was that I would pretend to want to have a look, and then with a brush full of tar paint concealed behind my back, I would give it a full daub when in full view. There was always a can of the sticky black stuff around somewhere. It was the crude basic tar paint—Black Naphtha—used for fishing punts, and therein lies the nub of this tale.

So when I called out, "Hey, Big J, let's have a look at your treasure," which he called it, concealing the loaded brush behind my back, he came over as innocent as a lamb and drew the monster from inside his pants, exposing the one-eyed, engorged, purple-like head with a great smirk of pride on that red face of his. Quick as a flash, I gave the top, a full helping of the tar paint. The commotion was terrible.

It must have been burning like mad as he ran around the yard in sheer agony of pain. He chased me at first, but the burning sensation was so great that he had to put it under the stand pipe. We watched in some mirth and trepidation as he eased the sting on his subsiding member, the tap issuing its blast of icy water to numb his digit. He shouted dire threats of horrors to come that were going to befall me.

Then there were times later, when he thought he would share the pleasure of his treasure, and gather his "men," as he called these babes, at the back of his dad's field and teach them things which they would discover anyway, but in the fullness of time.

He would organise special competitions for those he considered on the threshold of manhood. And being ever helpful, he wanted to give them a demonstration of what it was all about. After all, was he not the big chief with, by far, the biggest tomahawk?

His idea of a competition wasn't quite the norm. When I first saw him showing the young boys what to do, I wondered what on earth he was doing, but I didn't have to wonder for very long.

He had assembled the then innocents in a circle and started doing his usual trick, displaying his pride and joy. Again, I thought, what a whopper.

He then started to do things with it and told us we'd get to do the same. His got bigger and bigger and it seemed to change colour and then he turned away with a strange look on his face and he abruptly put it from sight saying, "That's what you've got to do with it. Practice when on your own, and you'll like it. I do it a lot."

That was how the competitions came about, because it wasn't very long before the children, or most of them, had become quite adept at deploying their treasures in their differing stages of development and really enjoying the experience.

One day Big J said that we must have a competition to see who could do it the quickest. He assembled us in a circle once again. He made us get out our varying digits and have them at the ready. Some of the boys, like me, would pretend, but really wanted to do it just the same. He would shout, "Fingers at the ready! Go!"

Then, after a brief hesitation, there was a general hive of industry as we applied ourselves with varying degrees of enthusiasm. The bigger boys were well away and enjoying themselves. Pretty soon, it was obvious that there was going to be only one winner as Big J brought his gusher forth, shouting, "Look! Look at all that stuff!" Then, looking at the younger ones, he commented, "Very soon you'll be able to do the same.

It comes with practice," and he laughed uproariously at his own joke and, not least of all, at those who couldn't quite make it. It made some of us feel a bit inadequate. I suppose it was nothing unusual. Innocent children growing up have done it since time began.

Big J and Sarah

One day, Brian the overseer had left us, as he had to go to the cattle auctions and deal with that aspect of the farm business. It was now Big J's chance to have a bit of sport with me.

The overseer had told us to be industrious and work hard until he got back. He had said this on occasions previously and usually got back at finishing time, being well refreshed with a glass or two of the black stuff.

"I expect you to have this field finished by the time I return." He looked up at the sky. "Remember, God is watching you."

Away he went, leaving us, seemingly without supervision. Big J came over, and I told him he was ugly, which started the chase. He chased me at full stretch and nearly caught me. Big J was running as hard as he could, but I had the edge and the advantage of fear which could lend wings. The very young Sarah kept shouting, "Quicker, quicker, or he'll catch you." Her concern made it all worthwhile. Eventually, he was exhausted and sat down.

I did likewise at a safe distance from him. I taunted, "Big J is Ugly Ginger."

"I'll get you, Mal." He jumped to his feet and made a last-ditch effort but failed just as I sped from his grasp. I kept ahead and he had to sit down again, exhausted from his efforts.

I sat down also, once again, keeping a suitable safe distance from him. He looked at me so grimly.

I said, "I'm sorry for calling you ugly."

"You will be. Just you wait."

"You've got no strength left. I could beat you now if we wrestled. You're too slow."

He was a lad who nature was making too big for his years. He couldn't comprehend the man frame he'd been given as a child. He was now in a man's body with all its desires being controlled by a child's brain. He was nearly twice my size and weight, but there was something nice about him that made it clear that he was not responsible for some of his actions, and I liked the way he protected the girls, especially Sarah, from school bullies and such.

While I relaxed at full stretch, he caught me off my guard and surprised me with a quick move, managing to grab my foot. He was now trying to flatten me into the earth as we wrestled, his full weight on top of me. I bit his bottom and made him yell. He then got hold of my privates and I got a hold of his. It was pure agony but I knew I could bear it just that second longer than he. It brought tears to my eyes. The pain was excruciating.

I wouldn't be able to walk properly for a week. I worried about it ruining me for the rest of my life. I think he secretly respected me for bearing the pain and not giving in first. Sarah was watching with more than a little interest as we struggled. She shouted, "Stop, stop," and, with childish laughter, emptied the water pale over our contorted bodies and saved me from further punishment.

Big J and I looked at her and both knew that all our fighting was about her. We didn't exactly know why or what for. At least I didn't, but Big J might have had the advantage in that respect, and I remembered when I'd peeped through the crack in the barn door when he was with Molly. He was horse-playing with her in a way I didn't know about, but wondered at. I'd like to have played with Sarah that way. While thinking on these heady matters, I was resolved to be with Sarah after work in the fields. She was now some way off among the stalks talking to Molly.

I moved nearer to Jim in the furrow.

"Jim, I want to take Sarah for a ride on Cecil when we finish and we'd like to be on our own."

"No you don't. She's my girl."

"She's not."

"I've a good mind to—"

"Now be careful, I was only suggesting. Come on, give me a chance. I want to be with her on her own for a change, without you always being around. Why don't you go with Molly?"

"I want Sarah, not Molly. Why don't *you* go with Molly, she likes you a lot. Anyway, I know what you're up to, and I'm going to ride on Cecil with you and Sarah or else."

"It's my horse. I'm in charge."

"It's not your horse. It's your dad's and you're taking unfair advantage. I tell you what, the short straw gets Sarah."

"No, she's coming with me. You've already had a start on me with Molly Brown when I saw you through the barn door."

"You were spying on me."

"No, I wasn't. You told me to look at how you got Molly to hold your treasure."

Big J, ignoring my last remark, was shouting to Sarah, "Is your sister really going to be married?"

Without waiting for an answer he continued, "I heard you got into trouble for showing off in the gym."

Sarah replied, "The teacher told me I was immodest because I jumped over the wooden horse without my gym slip on, and when I got home, my mother was cross. She said that she couldn't be buying us all gym slips."

Big J laughed wickedly and looked at Sarah. "We like to watch you and Molly when you're jumping. Don't we Mal?"

I nodded in an uncomfortable shyness and made no reply.

Big J guffawed and wasn't thinking of their sporting prowess. By way of reply, he ran over to where Cecil was quietly grazing and shouted, "Come on, Cecil, as he jumped onto his back. "Steady boy."

He was now astride Cecil and I was shouting as I ran, "What do you think you're doing? Throw him, Cecil, throw him."

Big J dug Cecil gently in the ribs with his heels and cantered down the field, grabbing Sarah in his strong arms. He swung her up in front, the way I'd shown her. I was mad with rage. "What are you doing?" she gasped in surprise.

He whispered to Sarah, "It's all right. Mal will catch us up later."

I started to run after them, and was in their wake as they came to the shallow crossing in the river. It was then that Cecil did his blackmail bit by stopping mid-stream. They didn't have a piece of carrot or sugar did they?

So he just stood there. I ran up to the stream and whistled at Cecil who turned around and saw me holding a juicy piece of carrot. Cecil moved fast as he turned, and Big Jim fell off as Sarah barely hung on 'til he came to me and received his bribe. Big J is now in the water and going mad.

"Gee up, boy, gee up." I was now astride with Sarah and wasn't going to wait for Big J. "Come on boy." And then shouting at Big J, "You're a rotten big bully for trying to take Cecil and Sarah."

He was bedraggled and wet after his immersion. I circled him for a while and Sarah said, "We can't leave him like that. We've got to light a fire and get him dry." She sounded very concerned and it annoyed me, although he did look a sorry sight.

I said, "All right, we'll light a fire."

After lighting the fire we sat and looked at the river while Cecil nuzzled his head to mine in search of more goodies.

He must have wondered about our antics and thought what strange creatures we humans were. As the fire blazed, the steam rose in vapour from Big J's clothes, a warm breeze helping the process. As he shivered a little in his underpants, I whispered to Sarah. "Let's go now while we have a chance. We won't be long."

He couldn't do anything but look at me in fury as I helped Sarah swing up onto Cecil and we moved off. I grinned and whispered into her ear, "It's all worked out nicely, what with Jim getting wet and me with you."

I took from my pocket a large ripe plum, which I'd wrapped in baking paper. Miraculously, it was still whole. "I've saved this for you."

She took a bite, offering the other half to me. It was the half with the stone. Cecil was cruising at about five knots and the entire world seemed a perfect place as we munched in unison. It was like a form of communion. Cecil could hear the munching and asked himself the question,

"Why aren't I munching too?" His pace slowed to a halt. In answer to his silent blackmail, I pulled another piece of carrot from my pocket, and we all masticated in harmony as we resumed normal speed.

All heads were now leaning forward, at a mind bending speed, as our charger stepped up the pace to about five knots. We munched in different keys as Cecil was given, yet another tooth sweetener. The undulating motion rubbed our bodies against each other with Sarah's face close to mine. Oh, why couldn't this heaven go on forever? The caress of our cheeks and the contact of her so close to me was pure bliss, as I experienced parts of me moving that I couldn't control, nor did I want to.

She broke my joyous reverie. "Wasn't Jim sneaky, trying to run off with Cecil and me?"

"He just wanted to be with you. I'd told him earlier, that I wanted to be with you and he was jealous."

She smiled and once more basked in her dream of the knights of old, jousting for her fair hand.

She said, "I suppose he likes me."

I laughed. "He lost the battle on account of Cecil and the river."

At length after an hour, she said, "I think we ought to get back. His clothes will be dried by now."

I nodded reluctantly.

Even at her tender age, she had evolved a certain philosophy about relationships. After all, there were times when she needed Big J as a form of protection in the school and the fields.

She enjoyed the luxury of having such a Galahad running around at her beck and call, and if you could have two, so much the better.

I said, "I want to be with you on my own without Big J always being around."

"I know, Mal, but sometimes, you're a bit strange with your innocent face. You make me so shy sometimes. I mean, you're not like the others, although I like you because you're so gentle and kind."

Even at that age I'd accepted the fact that I was different. I don't know why, but it didn't seem to bother me much, because I was not aware at that tender age of the way the world would think of me in later life.

I whispered in her ear as we sat astride Cecil, who I firmly believe used to listen to our talk and knew everything that was going on.

"On Thursday, we could slip away at midday break. No one would notice. I mean, we could wait until Brian leaves the field and goes to the fair. He's always back late from the fair. They say there are some fish in the river just now."

"Do you think we wouldn't be missed? We could make sure that we were back before he returned." Her voice sounded anxious.

"Even if we're found out, I think it'd be worth it to be with you, Sarah."

She smiled as we squeezed tighter together on Cecil's broad back. She asked, "What about Big Jim?"

"Not again. Why does he have to come? I want to be with you on my own. Why can't it be just you and me?"

"It will look better if we take him and Molly along. There'll be more to spread the blame. Especially as we are going to the river, it won't look so bad if we're found out."

I could reluctantly see the sense in what she said. "I suppose so."

The price of Big J's friendship came very high. She broke in on my thoughts, and reminded me. "He'll be dry by now."

As we neared the spot, Big J came running up shouting at us. "What kept you so long?" Then he smirked as he said, "We could have some fun while Brian's away."

Innocents in a Rain Dance

We were not supposed to talk at our work and, for the most part, toiled some distance apart to stop us from doing so. They were careful not to encourage any lack of industry. I loved those rare moments when Sarah worked in the same furrow with me. There was no distinction made between the girls and the boys. They were expected to do the same work. Needless to say, whenever the opportunity presented itself, we would chatter away like little monkeys. There would be laughter and banter that somehow relieved the tedium and helped us to get through those days when we should have been at play.

There is the memory of a very hot day when it started to rain heavily. We were at the farthest end of the big field, away from the shelter. The steam rose up from the wet stalks and the hot soil.

I said, "Can you feel those large drops coming down? They're warm."

"So they are," Molly laughed. "It's been so hot—"

Sarah interrupted, "I read about hot rain and the monsoons in a book. It told about how the people wait for months for the rains to come, and when it does, they do a rain dance. It seems that they only get rain once during their year, when it seems to never stop."

"That's a long time." I said as the rain got heavier and increased in intensity. The drops were splattering off my face and going through my thin cotton shirt. Then Molly said, while looking at Big J, "Let's stay out in the rain. Let it come. Let us do a rain dance."

Sarah was laughing in her innocence and shyness, full of a very young, natural exuberance. Then staring hard at me, she said, "Come on, Mal, don't keep looking so strange."

I made no reply but she made me feel uncomfortable, and I know she didn't mean to. She continued, "In this book I was telling you about, there was a Sun God. I read all about him. When I told the teacher, she explained it all to me. Well, anyway, it was all about the natives who were so happy when the rains came, when the crops blossomed, and they did their rain dance to rejoice. I'll show you. Come on. Come on, Mal, don't be such a quiet one. Let me show you."

Very soon, little pools were forming in the clay between the furrows.

Big J and Molly started laughing and joined hands, making a circle, as if to dance around an imaginary figure. They started to jump up and down.

Sarah, the angelic urchin, was now one of God's children with the rain making her hair scraggly, unkempt but lovely.

The warm rain was washing our souls and baring our hearts as I started to jump about with the others. Even jumping about in the rain could be fun. "Come on," she was shouting, "jump about and dance. Hold hands, hold hands."

I thought that if Brian the overseer could see us now, he'd have a fit. We were afraid of him. When I thought of this, I jumped more in defiance to vent some spite. We were jumping around and flattening the furrows, and the rain was relentless and so warm.

We cavorted in our mock imitation of a rain dance.

No one seemed to be worrying in the least about how wet we were getting. I opened my mouth to drink the rain in and I swallowed and quaffed. Sarah was laughing and the mud was sticking to her and she stood on her hands and did cartwheels to demonstrate her gymnastic skills. Big J was staring and clapping his wet hands. She shouted at us, "Go on. Do it if you can."

I tried and fell over on top of her. So did Big J with the same result, but I think that he did it on purpose. How could I be enjoying rain so much? Was it because we were transgressing? We were sinning. We were acting like wicked little devils. But we were oblivious to everything as we danced in our fashion. We were little piglets rolling in the mud. She shouted with the laughter of innocence, "I'm wet through and through."

"So am I," I shouted back as I leaped and rolled. Molly stood on her head again as her wet cloths fell about her ears and seemed to form part of her body. Big J had a light in his eyes as he gazed fascinated at her white knickers being rained on with the raindrops wetting her all over, and her once oh-so-white knickers were not so white as they became splattered with wet earth clinging to her private body parts. She didn't seem to care, this rebelling little soul, fast maturing into womanhood.

I just kept staring, as if hypnotised for the moment, as I involuntarily shouted, "Stop standing on your head. You'll dirty your clothes."

I don't know why I said it, because I really wanted to watch and watch as Big J gaped with the curiosity of his emerging manhood. His hand was in his pants, and I knew what he was doing. Molly kept cavorting with her legs in the air. What madness possessed her? Even Sarah, who was watching in a daze of excitement, was so taken aback. What possesses a mere baby of yesterday, a child who wants to celebrate the very exuberance of life? Such joyfulness of being alive itself through the bountiful wetting rain, a celebration indeed of His rain which will make all growing things burgeon forth.

Sarah ran over to where Molly was unashamedly still dancing and rolling in the wet earth, and they, with the others, began rolling in the wet clay. They engaged in a playful wrestling match. Big J and I were gawking as they tumbled and rolled about in absolute uninhibited enjoyment of their young souls, so entwined.

Molly was shouting, "Come on, you're going to get your clothes off."

She pulled Sarah's wet knickers off and soon there were two white bottoms being stood on their hands. The other children were jumping around in their innocence, laughing and shouting. Then they got hold of me and were pulling my trousers off, and strangely I didn't care as I rolled with the others and soon they were all doing the same and letting their naked selves be washed by the warm cleansing rain.

In a sea of naked bodies dancing around in the circle, there could be no guilt. It was as if the heavy warming drops were washing all our sins away.

While this impromptu celebration of life was been given full rein, there loomed in the far distant landscape the figure of overseer Brian. I looked and could see that we would have to be away as fast as legs would go. Young children, pick up your clothes and run. Catastrophe is only minutes away. He's now shouting from the far end of the field. I knew even then that there'd be a price to pay. We gathered our things so swiftly and ran, tumbling and falling in our haste, putting as much distance as we could between him and us. My heart warmed to Sarah, and it was in that second, that fraction of a second, that I loved a bare blossom in the mud and would be entranced by the imagery forever.

There was much shouting in our wake which made us quake, but we ran and we ran. *Just keep running, make more distance, this way, through the hedge.* We were now quicker on the firm grass as we sped. He won't catch us or know which way we've gone.

We were exhausted as we arrived in the woods at the back of the field which belonged to Big J's da. We took shelter as our bodies shivered under the friendly trees.

It had stopped raining, and a strong sun cast its heat as we gathered some wood and soon had a fire blazing. The tall wet grass helped clean us a little, and we were like dishevelled witches in the fire's flickering and shadowy warming light.

Drying out is one thing, getting cleaned up is another, and we had far too many tell-tale signs of our mud-bath. All and sundry would be in trouble at their various abodes, while the tar soap would be much in use.

We will not remember the discomfort of wet clothes clinging and yet will treasure the moment for all time. Why will they find it so difficult to understand? Why will they exact pain from us, so that we'll remember the painful price that will forever remind us not to do it?

I would remember, all those years later, that Sarah was my queen in the embryo stage. Not discerning and yet desperately seeking in life's learning, as a little wet elfin muddy angel.

When I told them that I had slipped, losing my balance and falling into a muddy pool alongside the ditch, they didn't believe me. The chastening parental voice would smite many ears. Too many had fallen into the ditches and had all told the same tale.

The cross questioning voice, "You didn't get any money today? I know you didn't because instead of working you were misbehaving."

She continued, "So you fell into the ditch. It must have been a great day for falling into ditches. Young Sarah, I was told, also fell into a ditch and, so it seems, did all of you. Stand still and don't twitch. Muddy ditch eh? Get those wet things off, it's the standpipe for you, young Mal, and then it will be to your bed and you'll go without." Then she added, "I'll see to Cecil." I'm sure that as he was led away to his stable he gave me a sad look, as if he knew, I would suffer.

Punishment

Rueful days go by and the overseer Brian stands over us like some colossus who has the power of life and death in the lives of compromised souls. "Yes, sir, we are all very sorry and we promise that it will never happen again. Yes, we'll make good the flattened furrows."

I'll promise anything to get over the nightmare of retribution.

> For those who eat the food,
> Will never know
> Of the innocent toil
> That made it grow.
> Tall flowering stalks
> To a child so small
> Must tend the soil
> That fed us all.

Does nature also dispose her favours and give more to some? All things are the same and yet nothing's the same.

The swish of the admonishing cane will deliver the stroke—because you have erred you must suffer. You must not break their rules. When you do so, they must hurt you. Can't you understand that? You see, if they don't hurt you, then they've not set the example for the others. That's how they see it. Even those who didn't make the rules feel it incumbent upon them to uphold them, and part of that upholding is the infliction of pain.

Swish goes the cane as it transmits its sting which brings the tear. It causes such anguish of the physical and mental? They make you feel so full of guilt and resentment, as you suffer without demur. It's all so civilised, because no-one has to hold you forcibly, because that is also an inflexible part of their rules. Although frightened out of your wits, you are immobilised by the threat of worse to come. So take your suffering and, "Don't move your hand, boy. Keep it steady!" The peremptory command authorised by the black-frocked holy teacher and administrator of pain-givers.

Teachers and Headmasters, whether they wear the cassock or not, or whether they form part of any religious order, are all to do with the shaping of your mind for that big bad world you'll have to face when released from their stewardship.

Our Christian Brother, who in his own youth had had the strictures of a pure life drummed into him, was well aware that he must relay those Christian values to those who came under his path of guidance, in that he would make us whole and better Christians.

Our headmaster, Mr Aloysius Palliard, was a very thin, tall man of fifty years. His visage was of a sunken appearance, as if his jaws were about to cave in. Heavy horn-rimmed spectacles perched on a long hooked nose, gave one the impression that, when dusk would settle in of an evening, his molars might descend. He had the Christian Brotherhood dogma embedded into his very being. His whole purpose on this earth, he did believe, was to make us better human beings to face a life of work and toil, in the fear and love of Him, whom we must all follow by his shining example, according to the scriptures. He would always be addressed as sir. He was secretly known by the pupils as Brother McGhoul.

When you were considered to have erred on more than a venal scale—like committing what in their eyes was a mortal sin—you were required to visit him in his study. He wore that ghoulish expression as he were about to savour his work, as you bared your backside, to receive your punishment. He would take his time as he swished away at your rear, and you would never forget him.

Our class of twenty plus was a mixed, for the most part, collection of underprivileged souls who always stood very still for the pain-giver who also thinks he's a simple soul, who also honestly believes that he was shaping our lives for the better.

After the mud-dancing episode, it had been decreed that we had transgressed on such a scale that we would have to receive our punishment at the highest level.

The message had come in from the fields that he was to make an example of those little devils who had behaved so shamefully. Make them bend to receive the pain to make them learn and to know that they must not roll in the mud. They must not do rain dancing when there is so much work to be done.

While other children played with their toys and dolls we cavorted in the mud. I was so worried about Sarah, whom I knew would suffer worse than I, because she would be ashamed when the others learned about what they had done. I feel for her in her suffering as those little angels were not excused the cane. Perhaps not as badly as we, as administered by Headmistress Kelly and not as many strokes, but they suffered. I, on the other hand, didn't care what they thought about me, because I had accepted deep down that it would always be thus.

From the "Torture Chamber," as his study was known, came the sound of *swish*, *swish*, as McGhoul applied himself zealously to his task of shaping our young souls.

"Stand still, boy." The miracle is that I can practically daydream and wonder about it all as

I accept the inevitable. Was it my fault that she shed her knickers? Did I ask her to do it? I didn't say, "Take your knickers off and dance in the field or wrestle in the mud." Instead of cursing the rain, somehow in our simplicity, we had blessed it.

Without it, none of us would be here. Nothing would grow and that would be the end of it all. Children should not express joyousness and certainly should not roll about in their natural state, or should children, or ladies-to-be, have their legs sticking in the air doing handstands.

We are taught by pain and reward. How can you tell very young children that it wasn't nice to throw your clothes off? It's difficult to explain and leaves too many questions unanswered. Innocents know nothing of any other implication.

We were guilty of such joyous free expression of life itself, which they would never comprehend. We had loved what we did to such an extent that it bordered on the blasphemous in their conditioned eyes, because they were taught to see only through the taboos of their own lives.

How can I think about all this and let it race through my mind as I feel the sting of the swish. Can the wielder of the instrument look into a child's mind? I don't hate him. He frightens me and yet I'm not frightened so much of him as when he repeats, "Stand still, boy."

And after, as I sit in my seat at the back of the class with the pain surging, I wonder at it all. I'm looking down the classroom and The Christian

Teacher is following my involuntary gaze. He is also looking at Sarah who is really suffering.

It's her pain which is causing me grief, as I suffer for us both. Why should everyone in our class have to gaze upon our suffering? The term public flogging is alien and yet in our simple little school, one was invariably caned in front of the class for what they considered minor offences, except in special circumstances when the sin was considered of such magnitude that you had to be dealt with at a higher level.

There were certain proclivities, or perhaps perversions might be more fitting, which at an early age were a mystery to comprehend. McGhoul used to take such a long time about the whole business, as he would make sure that he positioned your bottom precisely, so that it faced the window and had more light thrown on the object of his attention. He would comment with a sadistic laugh, "Come on, boy. Show your backside to the window and let's have more light upon the subject, ha, ha," making that dreadful ghoulish laugh. Then as your head was cast down toward the floor he could be heard swishing his collection of canes until he'd selected the one for the task. It was all intended to make the ordeal more painful mentally, and it succeeded.

He would pause between each stroke and make certain noises, not unlike grunts of stifled satisfaction, and you dare not move until he had finished, when, at length, he would seem to gaze at his inflicted red lines across one's rear, and say, "You may now stand up, boy."

Thus, you were told that your session of hurt and humiliation was over.

Brian the overseer would now be somewhat placated at learning of our punishment and would look at us with a hidden smile of, "That'll teach you scallywags."

When next we were under his command, you had better behave. He would have discussed the goings on at length with his drinking pals at the local hostelry over several pints of the dark stuff, while holding forth to all and sundry.

"Oh, Lord, save us. And what are we coming to when children throw off their clothes and dance and roll in the mud like animals and shout and sing wild songs. It's a blasphemy."

On one occasion I was due to receive six of the best for another offence, like when we fished instead of helping with the harvest. On this occasion, he seemed to take forever with my backside in the air, bent over his desk. Even at that age I could feel his gaze upon my person while he savoured his work. Bringing God into his work was in my young mind, the ultimate obscenity, as he would say on finishing his labours, "God bless our efforts and may our labours make the minds of His children pure." Then he would take some time to adjust his own dress, before uttering in an imperious dismissive voice, "You may now stand up."

One time when I looked into his cavernous face, it was as if there were an empty space behind the thick lens of his spectacles. It was like looking into dark cavities.

McGhoul would be long remembered by many young boys. Some would remember him forever. The last time I was brought to his office, his voice ran thus, "Ah yes, ah yes, young master Mal. 'It's you again. I understand it's to be six strokes. Very well, pull them down and bend over the desk with your back to the window. Yes, well down as I've shown you. Now just stay very still and don't move, boy. Stay quite still."

Then his usual ritual of selecting which cane he would use. I could hear the swish, as he had his usual practice swings, which nigh made the experience unendurable, as I anticipated what was to come.

Then his voice again, "Look at the floor, boy."

It was imperative to be still and make not a sound, while receiving his painful bounty. If you moved, it earned you another stroke and sometimes he said you moved and gave you another one anyway.

"Now remember, young Mal, stay at your work and always help to bring in His bountiful harvest. The work on the land is a most holy gift to us, outside of the church itself. Playing truant and fishing in Murphy's part of the river is a mortal sin. It is the taking of fish that are not your property and is stealing."

While he ranted on about stealing the fish, I couldn't help thinking of them swimming all that way across the ocean. Did anybody own them?

Then, "Back to your class boy and learn to behave."

The school bell is ringing. Sarah's asking me anxiously and concerned, "Does it hurt much?"

In my bravest voice, "Not too much."

"I feel terrible. It's my entire fault and also Molly's. It was all because of us doing the rain dance. If we hadn't done it, it wouldn't have been so bad."

"It's not your fault. It's Big J's and mine, because we loved what you did." I was thinking that the men must always take the blame. I managed to smile.

She said, "When I got home, they put me in the bath and scrubbed me."

"You were lucky."

She continued. "My mother said that she wasn't ever going to let me go to the fields again, and that I was a disgrace."

I could only comment, "She doesn't mean that. Last month she was so pleased when you brought her your hard earned shillings. She'll soon forget."

"Oh, I don't know."

It was then that she kissed me on the cheek. At that moment of pure heavenly bliss, it was all worth it, and then out of her satchel she took a piece of her mother's cake.

What a treat as I walked on air. We munched and said nothing. I loved her as only a child can.

Big J's bottom seemed impervious to the cane or strap. His voice intrudes into my heaven as he comes into view and shouts, "How are all the mud-larks?"

Sarah winced while seeming to ignore his question. She whispered, "I'll see you tomorrow after school."

I looked into her face full of joy, as with a note of defiance I said, "We could go fishing Thursday, while Brian makes his usual visit to the fair and Mulligans. He is never back until late. We'll not be missed."

"Oh, yes, why not?" she answered in defiance. "We can fish near the bend under cover from the trees."

Big Jim was musing as he said, "I'll be glad when we can help with the hay. We can have some more fun then." Big J had an uncanny way of seeing things ahead. Whatever punishment ensued as a result of his actions, didn't seem to bother him.

Sarah's mother's voice from afar, "Come, girl, why are you so late?" She looked past me, as if I weren't there. Cecil and I plodded on into the dusk.

Neither of us was in a hurry to part. Our heads were close as we talked like horse and human are apt to do when exchanging their most private thoughts.

When I put him into his stall with his water and feedbag, I gave him an extra piece of sugar and the carrots of course. I must never forget that.

I could hear a mother's tired voice penetrating the dusk and my thoughts. "Daydreaming again? Why are you so late? You never seem to be in a hurry to come home."

I gave Cecil a gentle nudge. He'd done his share of work for the day and now he was duly fed, stabled and watered. He nuzzled up close to my face.

"Good boy, Cecil. Go on, why not have another piece." He said thanks by way of giving my ear a soft nibble. I knew he understood everything as I would tell him my thoughts.

"The day after tomorrow, we'll fish and who knows what else?"

Later at my bedside, I said prayers, Matthew, Mark, Luke and John, God Bless the bed that I lie on. And I added, and Cecil and Sarah and even Big J and also, "Please God, let it be nice and sunny tomorrow."

As I whispered my little prayer, I knew that we would have to suffer if our sins and omissions were to be discovered.

Then to Bed

In the warmness of my bed I tended to dream about everything. Being in charge of Cecil had given me some power over Big J. In my flights of fancy, I was on my big white charger and Sarah was my princess. I would secretly make plans to be away with her and take her to faraway lands to a golden palace, make her my queen and spend the rest of our days together in heavenly bliss. I would daydream about it for hours and picture Cecil with white mane flowing and Sarah holding on tight, as we sped like the wind over hill and plain to make all our dreams come true.

There was only one snag. It was Big J. I could see him as the obstacle in my way. He would bar our path, hold the bridge. He would fight me to the death before he'd let me take the fair princess away. In my little world, Big J was looming too large in my plans and our school wasn't big enough for both of us. He would have to be dealt with, but how? A child's mind to be filled with such dreams was pure fantasy, as I confront him and say, "This school isn't big enough for both of us."

"Oh, yeah?"

"Yeah."

"What ya' goin' to do 'bout it?"

"Conkers behind the hay shed after school."

"Who'll be your second?"

"Sarah."

"Can't have her. Better have Molly."

"Okay, Molly. What's the difference? I'm goin' to get ya' anyway."

"Oh, yeah?"

"Yeah, an' you can take that for a start."

Stars abounding as I'm awakened by a mother's voice, "You'll be late again, if you don't shake yourself and get up."

As I rub the sleep from my eyes, I'm thinking, which is the worst, the school or the fields? As I wait to use the washroom, the cold voice of the father of the house, "Use the stand pipe in the yard, boy."

Outside, it's summer. The wind is fresh and the water is cold. Then back inside, there's a plateful of porridge and, as I daydream, comes the motherly voice, "Eat your breakfast. You'll be late again."

The Soup

As I'm leaving: "Here's your flask of soup."

Ah, yes, the soup. The memories of a child's taste buds indelibly printed in soup. The pot was so large and heated over glowing embers to simmer day after day, with everything in and nothing wasted. Never to spill a drop.

She was the great soup maker of all time, always tending the never-ending brew, the great vessel, full of everything she could muster from the fields. The butcher always saved her a cow's head. It all went through a fermenting process, with the aroma floating round the old walls of a cottage which had become a house through the necessities of building on through time to accommodate progeny, mostly conceived while under the influence of the Black Stuff from the waters of St James Wells processed by one Arthur Guinness, who, singlehandedly, was the prime cause of many a large family being fruitful in the fear and love of Him in an obligation to multiply, as per His Book of The Faith and, of course, to create more customers for his brew and support of the Holy Fathers. To always be increasing His flock of believers and potential imbibers of his product.

There would be the usual ritual of the first tasting and all savouring in anticipation and always on a Saturday when the informal ceremony would take place. Muslin cloths would sift and strain. It was the kind of soup which you nearly had to eat for the most part. With a world war raging, some were very lucky to have, as so many went without.

A child's memory will always retain and savour those fond tastes of yesteryear. The industry of it all. The loving tender care in its preparation, will never be forgotten.

Soup-filled, to bed,
and prayers to be said.

My friend of the "Tar Top," Big Jim, loved her soup. He was the soup king. When invited to partake, he would be on the second bowl before I'd hardly started mine. No matter how hot she served it, it made no difference to him. We thought he must have a leather tongue, what with the soup and father's game expeditions into the adjacent mountains of our fair land, as a provider for her pot.

When he would sally forth, and when luck would smile, our pot would receive the results of his labours in the shape of an unlucky duck or rabbit, or even a wild pigeon and sometimes a stray chicken. Nothing that moved would be spared

It all went into the mix of the magic cauldron to sustain those who were so dependent on its contents. We all had our own individual bowl. Mine showed the marks of much usage from its travels into a child's unknown, not least of all the fields and boat and more fields.

It bore the scars of much usage in the chipped enamel. If you didn't have your bowl to hand at all times you might fail to receive your share of the sustenance.

If it was extra nice, she'd have a little more than a taste. Then it would be dispensed. A mother's ritual you might say.

Spying on Sister Monica

Sister Monica was some years older than I. I envied her age, with full permission to stay out until it was getting dark. Her friend Jill, from across the way, also had similar privileges. The guidelines were that they were never to lose sight of each other and to be in by ten o'clock at the very latest in the summer. This could be a bit difficult when going to the local dance. On one particular evening they'd been given a special extension. They could stay out till eleven.

I said, "Aren't you lucky being able to go out in the evening?"

"Well, I'm older than you, and besides, I am trusted. We're not like little pigs who don't know how to behave and roll in the muck and take their clothes off with little girls, and then have to be given the cane."

She continued, "Like we don't jump about in fields, do we? We know how to behave. We don't play truant from school and go fishing." She continued, "We can be trusted to be left out on our own."

She sounded so grown up and repeated our mother's comments concerning troublesome children.

My inquisitive mind was always curious about what they did when they went out together? Is a curious child's mind an excuse for spying on your sister?

I decided that I would follow them at a safe distance. I'm sure my dear Sarah would never have approved. It was to be the first of my many spying and Peeping Tom sallies that would become such a part of an inquisitive quirk in character and forever be a part of my life. There was, even then, some part of a malfunction, which gave me a thrill observing the actions of others, when I should not have done so.

So when I was supposedly tucked up in my bed, I'd kept my clothes on underneath the quilt and waited. When I peeped through the window and saw her leave the house, I crept down the back way, via an old friend, in the shape of the oak, overhanging the ledge. It had been there for so many years, long before any of us had come into the world. It had often been a friend in my innocent escapades.

I watched her go across the field to Jill's cottage and saw them continue on together. It was getting dark as I kept a safe distance in their wake while they made their way along the dark lane, with its canopy of overhanging shrouding branches. After about half a mile, I was surprised to see that they didn't turn left to go toward the village hall where the dance was taking place. Instead, they turned the other way, toward the woods. I followed, well hidden by the abundant foliage and feeling more curious than ever.

In the darkening woodland, lit by a full moon dappling through the trees. I could dimly make out two people coming towards them and hearing their greetings, "Hello, Tim."

"Hallo, Jill."

The penny dropped. *Ah,* they were meeting boys. Oh, well, well. Although I felt guilty at spying on my sister, it was the pure inquisitiveness of a growing lad. What was I expecting to discover?

So there was my sister Monica and her friend Jill walking with the boyo's who had brought their bikes. The boys wheeled the bikes along as they walked arm in arm with the girls. Now, dare I go closer? I must not. Discovery would cost me dear. I was filled with a sense of guilt at what I was doing. But I didn't feel too guilty at the time. My curiosity was too strong. It got the better of the enormity of what I was doing, as it did in later life.

I was still keeping my distance when they turned into the woodland leading to the lush meadow of farmer Ben Doyle. They left their bicycles propped against a tree. As I crept through the undergrowth I could hear their voices. I kept working my way stealthily under cover of the foliage and, for a moment, I thought I had lost them. I crawled along almost on my belly for some time. When quite close at hand, I could hear the rustling movement in the tall meadow grass. I stopped and held my breath. I raised my head, and what a surprise. It took a few seconds for me to comprehend the scene, or understand it, but very near to me at close range—I could have nearly touched them—were two great thighs raised with a man in between. The thighs flashed white in the moonlight, spread apart.

Who did they belong to? Jill or my sister? Such relief when I heard a soft voice whisper, "You do love me, don't you, Sean? Are you sure you love me? You do, don't you?" And a man's grunt at the intent of his industry made me feel strange all over, as I crept slowly away, making sure I made no noise, with a mixed feeling of guilt and relief.

I was so frightened for fear of discovery, although fascinated, but inwardly very jealous at the freedom they were allowed. As I came to where they'd left their bicycles, the quicker my step became, and I was quite out of breath as I ran and ran. I couldn't get the picture out of my mind.

I climbed up my friendly tree. Back in my bedroom, I was throwing my clothes off and got safely back in my bed. As I lay there in my fantasy world, I imagined all sorts of things about Monica, Jill, Sarah, and Molly. I prayed to Him for forgiveness, in my wicked act of spying. And the night was full of what the day was about.

In my world of growing up and discovery, sleep and dream, were never far away. As I lay there in my warm bed, I felt so guilty for spying on their secret romance. Then sleep, the sleep that gradually wafts the mind of the very young and curious, so soundly into another world of escape and fantasy.

Asleep between her sheets which she had scrubbed so white. I dreamt of what I had seen and what it is like to be growing and growing but never knowing. I dreamt of little elves and children at play with Big Jim, naked, drying by the fire, and both of us innocently lusting for Sarah in pure snowflake innocence. I dreamt about Cecil and how we constantly exploited him as our ship of the fields to carry us into our dreams, while trying to make them come true, and my sister and Jill, their appetites so fulfil.

At the table next morning, I kept staring at her to see if I could see anything different. She said quite suddenly, as if reading my thoughts, "Ma, make Mal stop staring at me. What's the matter with him? He's not going to have another one of his funny turns. You'd think I was an apparition."

I asked quietly, with malice, "Did you enjoy your evening at the dance?"

She spluttered and nearly spilled her cup of tea. "Yes I did, and what's the matter with you this morning? Stop staring at me like that."

"The cat may look at the king."

Then a mother's stern tongue: "Run along, run along. You're late."

Harvest Fish and Molly

It was harvest time, a time when young children on long holidays from school worked in the fields.

I made my way along to Cecil's stable. At one time, in a fit of industry, Jim and I had painted it all the colours of the rainbow. We'd hung baskets of flowers outside to make it look pretty.

Cecil nodded his head when I came through the half door. He always seemed to be waiting and ready for me. I gave him his first lump of the day, as I put the bridle on him. He was happy and contented and seemed to smile the way horses do when they bare their teeth.

We were in mobile mode as we went *clippity clop* down the lane to where Jim was waiting at the corner.

"You're late as usual."

He grabbed my arm and swung up behind me. I don't know what it was about Jim being on a horse with me. We never seemed to be at one. He always wanted to take over. We sometimes carried three and even four children squashed together. There was sufficient room when we squeezed up close against each other. Jim would sometimes stretch his arms past me when Sarah was up front and hold her hand, which upset me. She didn't seem to object to it. I did. I would sit back on the horse to force him back into a precarious position. He would yell, "What do you think you're doing? I'm nearly falling off."

He would then get the general idea that I wasn't in accord with what he was doing. After all, was I not the captain and in command? The sole commander, navigator and captain of the good ship, "Cecil."

Jim broke in on my thoughts, "As soon as Brian goes to the fair, we'll be off."

"Oh, yes."

Jim casually added, "We're to meet Molly later."

"Maybe I'll get another peep at you, Jim." I laughed and then he nudged me in the back and I nearly fell off."

I elbowed him back and, in the ensuing fracas, we both fell off. It seemed a miracle that we never got hurt. Just bruises of the very young. We picked ourselves up and remounted. I didn't know at this stage that Jim had spoken to Molly at length, telling her that I wanted to be with her on her own, and that I was very fond of her but too shy to tell her.

I could see Sarah. It warmed my heart just to look at her with her fair hair brushed back over her shoulders. She was as pretty as a picture with those lovely blue eyes. I jumped down from Cecil. "Hurry," she said, "My dad will be along shortly."

I helped her up on to Cecil, and her elder sister, who was now a young woman and quite shapely, came into view. She held her nose in the air. Ever since she left school and got the job in the post office, she wouldn't deign to acknowledge our existence. I thought of the other night when I'd watched in the long grass and her legs were in the air.

"Your sister is very pretty, Sarah." Jim said, by way of an adult paying a compliment. Then he teased, "I think she's prettier than you." Big J was making fun.

I retorted, "Shut up, Jim. Sarah is far prettier. At least I think so."

"Thank you, Mal."

I gave her a little squeeze which she returned by holding my hand.

Jim smiled at Sarah and said, "I was only joking," and added, "I've got some of my dad's special poteen, and I've put it in my water bottle."

I replied, "That's the stuff that makes me cough and splutter. I don't know how you drink it."

"Anyone who doesn't take a drop is a sissy." He gave that wicked laugh of his.

"I'll drink it with you, Jim," Sarah cooed.

Jim gave Cecil a prod in the ribs, and he gave a start and took off in a short burst, and then stopping suddenly, nearly throwing us all off, as if to say, "Don't do that or I'll start playing rough."

He wouldn't move until the bribe was paid.

"Now see what you've done. You've upset him."

"All right, I'm sorry. I won't do it again."

As we arrived at the field of our labours, the admonishing voice smote the air. Brian was in control mode. "You children, late again. Nothing changes. You'll never learn. Come on. There's lot's to do. Grab those forks." He set us to work. No time for talking.

Later, prayers would be said in thanks to Him for the richness of the harvest. Sarah had been called away to do some chores at the big house. Jim and I liked helping with the wheat, which was a pleasant change from the furrows. Slowly, so slowly, the clock arrived at lunchtime and Jim whispered, "It won't be long now."

I looked over and saw Sarah coming back from the big house, where, instead of being employed in the fields, she was often given tasks of a domestic kind.

Brian rang the bell for the break and was thinking and looking forward to an extended liquid lunch at Mulligans, while listening to the craic and sipping at length with his peers away from labours of the soil. Suitably lubricated, they would go on to the cattle fair, where they would sup some more of that world famed brew, courtesy of the bountiful waters from the blessed liquid of Saint James Wells.

Brian's voice droned above, "Make sure, you're all back here promptly at two o'clock sharp."

We made our way to where Cecil was peacefully grazing and, having mounted our beloved steed, cantered through to the other field where Molly was waiting. She was helped up by grabbing Jim's arm and we were close up, four aboard. Cecil stopped and was given his extra fare.

He munched and re-started. "We'll have to go to where we've hidden the sticks," Jim said.

Molly was delighted. She cried, "Oh, I was looking forward to today."

"Me too," Sarah said.

Molly was all aglow, as she asked me, "I hope you'll show me how to catch a fish, Mal. Sarah told me that you are very good at knowing where they are lying in the river."

"I've been lucky once or twice."

I was flattered by the way she was paying so much attention to my prowess at fishing, as we arrived at the bend in the river where the woodlands came down to the water's edge.

"This'll be a good place. Murphy's Pool nearly always holds a fish, if they're in the river. There's plenty of cover at this point and there's no one about. But we must be constantly on the lookout."

I liked to sit on the bank and listen to the water cascading down over the rocks and look at the deep pools, never knowing what fish might be resting in their depths before battling the current to higher reaches to propagate its kind. The water looked so good, inviting us to cast our bread it would seem. The girls spread out our pieces, bread, cheese and apples. Mine was wrapped in a piece of linen. Jim and I were putting our basic rods together made from stringy saplings. The girls ate daintily while we munched. Jim took the poteen from his bag.

"Let's see who can drink without coughing."

If his dad knew that he had purloined some of his precious liquid, he would have been in trouble. We all had to have a sip and coughed and spluttered, that is, except Jim.

I got busy, as I fixed the hook with some white feather attached. I cast the line out over the flowing water and let it settle behind a big boulder, where I had been lucky in the past.

I twitched it about, to give it life as Molly sat down beside me and said, "I want to see how you do it, Mal."

"Don't make so much movement and stay back from the water."

I cast it again into the hole behind a boulder, where a fish might lie, before attempting the journey to higher water.

Sarah said to Molly, "Don't you want to sit with Jim?"

Jim chimed in. "No, Molly's all right with Mal. Sarah, you come down farther along with me and we'll try our luck down past the bend."

He took her by the hand and they walked further down the river bank. I was jealous and wanted to run after them.

"Molly said, "Leave them. I bet we'll catch more than them."

I tried to concentrate on the fishing. Some time elapsed as I cast and re-cast into the pool. I thought I saw a fish move and cast in front of its nose. Sure enough, he took the hook with the feather, and I tightened and hung on as he tried to streak up the pool. Molly grabbed my arm at the wrong moment and the line went slack—my prize was gone. She had not comprehended what had just happened and was shouting excitedly, "I knew you'd get one."

I was very cross and fairly shouted at her, "What in the name of all the saints, did you do that for?"

Sometime later, I got another tug and hooked another.

"Now keep quiet, Molly. Don't move. Stand by ready while I get it into the shallows, so I can drag it up the shingle, away from the water."

"Oh, yes, I know how to do that. My dad showed me."

Molly was excited and shouted, "I'm ready, Mal. I'm ready." She was waving the small handmade gaff about. The fish was a real fighter and it took some time before I had it near. I could see the flash of silver and it looked a good size. Molly was nearly out of her skin with excitement and so was I. Gradually, gradually, I got it to the surface and then, after a few minor mishaps, near the bank and onto the gravel. We'd got him! I grabbed it by the tail and, holding it very firmly, drew it up swiftly. In feverish excitement we looked at our prize. It was a good size grilse. I struck him on the head with a small rock and his soul flew to where good fish go in the after-life.

She was so excited and asked, "How much does it weigh?"

"It's about eight to nine pounds." I tried to be casual but could scarce conceal my own excitement and wanted to run down river to Sarah and Jim to tell them. But Molly had other ideas for her hero.

Jim had heard our shouting and came running up, bringing his dad's poteen. We had to have a sip to wet the fish. Molly liked the stuff and had several and didn't seem to cough or splutter. I thought that this was not the first time she had supped from Big Jim's bottle. She then threw her arms around me. "You're so clever, Mal."

I couldn't help thinking that Sarah hadn't come to see my fish.

As I'm thinking thus, Jim said, "I'll be getting back to Sarah," and he was off to be with her. Deep down I knew that Jim had put one over on me and had taken Sarah, who wouldn't even come up to look at my fish. I would have been even more upset if I had known the entire story.

Ill concealing my feelings I said to Molly, "Shall we go down and see how they're getting on?"

She replied dismissively, "I'm not worried about them. We'll see them later. I mean, aren't we after landing the great big fish. They've caught nothing."

"All right, we'll see if we can catch another and then we'll go down and—"

She interrupted, "You just want to see what they're doing. It's got nothing to do with fishing anyway. I mean, you really like Sarah and you don't like me."

She was now very upset and near to tears. I put my arm around her and then defiantly said, "I don't care what they're doing. I couldn't care less."

Molly said, in spiteful vein, "I hope he's putting his hand up her clothes."

"Don't say things like that, Molly. It's not nice."

"It's not nice, but that's what you're thinking. Jim always tries to kiss every girl. But he says he only loves two girls and that's Sarah and me. He can be an awful lot of fun to be with." She said the last bit with a glint in her eyes.

"All right, Molly, you needn't go on."

Then she said quite tenderly. "I do like you a lot, Mal, even though you are a bit strange, but nice." Then quite suddenly, "Come on, let's wrestle and see who's the strongest."

I thought that Jim's bottle must have gone to her head as she grabbed me and dragged me to the ground. She was much bigger than I and having got hold of my arm she says, "I'm going to get you to submit to Queen Molly. You must swear to obey me in all things. I'm going to keep you here, 'til you promise."

My heart quaked as I struggled with this young leviathan. She was the best girl wrestler in our school and could take on most of the boys and had made many of them submit, in more ways than one. Being on the very small side, I had no chance and there was no part of her that I could grab to level the contest. So I keeled over, and why not? I think some of the illicitly distilled liquid in Jim's dad's mixture had also affected me, and I thought there must be some way that I could win. Now she grabs my leg and throws hers across, pinning me to the ground. This heaving female is whispering close to my ear, "I don't want you to submit too soon."

I stuttered hoarsely, "You're strangling me."

"Come on. I'm not hurting. We're only playing."

"You might be playing, but even Big Jim doesn't play as rough as you."

"Come on. Fight back."

I thought she must weigh about two ton. I was so over-powered by this writhing creature. I tried to get her off, but I began to secretly enjoy the way she was pulling me about and moving across my body. My hand started to creep up the back of her dress and I started to pull at her knickers.

"That's not fair." But she didn't sound serious.

She pressed her hand into my groin, just like Jim had done when he wanted me to submit, but this was a lot different. It was gentle and had the desired effect of making me want her to leave it there, as I started to explore further among her rounded parts, with which I was keen to be familiar. It was electrifying. She laughed as she squirmed in enjoyment. She was totally in charge.

I was content to stay under her as I panted and puffed. In the throes of this new experience, I had forgotten about Sarah and Jim as I became happily submissive to this female and more aroused as she strove in some mysterious fashion to subdue and excite, moving herself all over my body. It wasn't long before I gurgled in an early traumatic fulfilment and felt my wetness, and all at once I wanted to tell her, "Molly, get off," but I didn't.

She started to laugh and that really worried me. I didn't like the way she was laughing. It was the laugh of a girl filled with the devil and Jim's bottle. She was fast becoming the queen to be fulfilled. I seemed to speedily recover from my first wet outburst and started to explore again as her face grew flushed with her own feelings and what her natural instincts desired. She didn't know it, but at that moment she had probably became my earliest queenly wetting experience.

As we lay there, she, very quiet, said, "Let's have another drink from Jim's flask," which he'd left on the bank. She raised the bottle and, after we shared some more of the burning liquid, was astride again like tons and tons of baby love bent on getting to the terminus. With the false courage of the firewater coupled with my desire, I was allowed to re-explore the further mysteries of the very young. Her breath started to come in gasps and sighs as she was whispering, "Do you think Sarah and Jim are wrestling like us?"

"I don't care," I lied.

"I love you, Mal."

The relentless movement of her body to and fro had me soon again experiencing another ecstatic haze and, once more, was wetting inside my clothes as she stopped and gasped, "Now wasn't that nice, Mal. Don't you love me just a little?"

"Yes, yes," I mumbled amid a mixture of strange emotions. She had obviously now decided to end the wrestling and was settling her dress which had been in some disarray.

"Do you still want to go and see the others?"

"Yes, but don't tell Sarah that we wrestled." As I said this, I wondered why I felt guilty.

"I won't if you don't." She kissed me and added as an afterthought, "Jim is older than you in so many ways."

She was now a little detached and I felt like the toy being put aside. It was at times like this that I could really envy Jim.

Cecil had been quietly grazing. I'm sure he didn't realise what young pups he transported at times. I nuzzled him and put a small carrot to his lips, and he put his head onto my shoulder as in a nodding, "Thank you, Mal."

Molly said abruptly, "I suppose you think I'm a bad girl, don't you?" Without waiting for an answer, she continued, "I know that you watched Jim and me when you looked through the barn door."

For some reason I thought back to when mother let me sit in the well of her skirt by the fireside. Her voluminous heavy tweed skirt made a kind of hammock for us cherubs to lie on, and I'd known the safety of her net as I'd slept within the confines, but today I thought that I'd now fallen forever from her folds.

Molly observed my faraway expression.

"What are you dreaming now, Mal?" She repeated her earlier comment, "You are a strange one at times, but you're nice and gentle."

I didn't answer and gave her an arm up behind me on Cecil. I gave him another piece and a gentle nudge with my knees as we moved out.

"Good boy," I whispered in his ear, and he gave a low whinny of a horse who was content.

It was getting late as we moved along the bank to where Sarah and Jim were.

Then suddenly Molly said in a chafing tone, "You're still bothered about them."

At that moment Jim came out from some cover along the bank and shouted, "Hello there yourselves."

"Had a good picnic? Catch anything?" I asked in a sarcastic tone.

He looked a bit ruffled. Maybe he'd been wrestling too! Sarah came towards us in an air of despondency. She looked a bit dishevelled and hung her head a little as she sensed my feelings. Why was I feeling so hurt?

"Come on," I said. "We'd better get going. Molly, you better sit up front and Jim and Sarah behind. Jim, you hold onto the bag."

Young angels gathered up their sticks and things, with the fish now in the sack bag. When fully laden, Cecil turned his head, and I bent forward and gave him his extra fare which I could hear him crunch quite audibly. We were quiet as we rode and then the silence was broken at length by Molly, "Wasn't that a lovely fish that Mal caught?"

I wanted to say that I thought it was the day of the one that got away, but instead, "You'd better say that you caught it, Jim, and I'll have half. You'll be able to explain it better."

"All right, Mal" Then he added, "You worry so much."

The story about the fish, when I had brought home my half with an air of innocence and childish pride, was the evidence they had against me that made them really suspicious, and I was indicted.

Then later on, when I was supposed to be at school, they came to the river where I was fishing. So when I was back at school, I was to be in receipt of further treatment at the hands of McGhoul.

More Cane and Revolt

Indelibly printed was the moment when I entered his punishment hole. It was like being in a hopeless dream, where there could only be one unpleasant and painful outcome. There had been a critical time warp from the time I had been with Molly and the very thought of him baring my bottom and exposing myself to his gaze, was too much. The resentment was boiling up inside me to a pitch where I was losing all control. I was surprised at the sound of my voice when I heard the swish of the cane as he exercised his arm in those dreadful practice swings. I screamed and kicked at him. I was in such a state that two senior Brothers of the Cloth had to come and hold me down. As I received the strokes, I still screamed and kicked and called him filthy names. I didn't care who heard. He struck me across the face, drawing blood from my mouth.

As I stood bleeding with my trousers around my ankles, the Ghoul seemed to savour the drama and the blood. I could only see his face as that of the devil himself.

He held the cane on high as if to threaten that if I made any more fuss, I would feel it again.

My mother had to be sent for. She, who knew her issue, also knew that it was already too late for anything to make any difference any more.

I was firmly cast in a mould that was forever of one who would not conform.

In the following months, Cecil and I (he was the only one who understood me) would cover miles in our solitude. I cried sometimes to myself as I sat astride this great loyal creature, who seemed to know everything.

Sometimes when back in his stable, we would sleep in the same straw. The resentment was building up all the time in a young body. It would always be there.

Assault

Then the final straw. I wouldn't go to school, but found my trusty stick in its hiding place and made my way to the river, where a most dreadful thing happened to me when I should not have been there, because I should have been at school. I was frightened when they learned about it.

How could I tell them that two horrible men had interfered and done awful things to me? Even now, it makes me feel sick to think about it. I was too frightened to tell them painful details, because, I repeat, I should not have been there and it would only have made it worse for me and caused a mother more pain. They would have blamed me, instead of getting the Garda to find those dreadful men.

It happened as I was casting my line and so absorbed that I didn't notice them at first. Then I heard one, the younger of the two, as he took hold of Jim's flask, opened it, and put his nose to the neck. He had a good smell and said to the older man, "It smells good, Tom. Want to try a drop?"

They were looking at me and smiling in a funny kind of way as they drank in turns. The older one grimaced with satisfaction and wiped his lips as he said to me, "So, you don't like school, and you like to have a drink with you when you go fishing, eh? What a man of the world you are."

And they both laughed and laughed at their own joke. Then the older one said, "It's not fair us having a drink and not inviting you to have one from your own flask." Then they held me as they stuck it into my mouth and made me swallow. I nearly vomited.

I was very frightened when the older one pulled my rod from the river and, winking at the other, who, having now emptied the flask, had thrown it into the swirling waters, said, "Let's show the chubby little humpty lad the woods where the leprechauns live."

The other started to laugh and grabbing an arm each they made me go into the woods with them. I was feeling very strange with the effect of the drink, and when they made me lie down on the ground I started to struggle and shout. The older one hit me on the side of head with something he'd taken from his pocket, and I must have passed out, but I knew what they were doing to me. They hurt me so much that I could hear myself scream. The man hit me hard again and the next thing I remember was waking up and all was quiet, except for the rain and then I realised that I had no clothes on.

It was now late and fast becoming dark. I started to cry and cry as I felt the pain from where I'd been abused. Blood was dripping from the side of my head. I screamed in mental and physical agony with the hopelessness of my situation. But there was no response from the lonely trees, just the sound of water flowing over the boulders in the river and the heavy rain coming down.

I eventually found my clothes lying around and put them on, wet as they were. I found my satchel, which was soaked with its contents. I made my way in absolute misery toward that place where I would be interrogated. Where else could I go? When they asked their questions, I just couldn't speak or answer them, except to mutter about men beating me up. I was so choked up with the dreadful experience of it all, that no matter what they did I just sat there numb and motionless, with all the querying faces around. They weren't faces of love and concern, but of anger and frustration at this child, who brought additional troubles while they strived in their hard working lives.

It was as if they would say, "How dare you have anything happen to you."

Then she stripped and bathed me, echoing all the time, how much trouble I was to them all, and as she wiped the congealed blood from my temple, she was crying, but when she saw the blood from my underpants where I had bled as a result of their most dreadful intimate assault on my most private area, she nearly had a fit.

She got the doctor immediately, who seemed very tired and overworked by his demanding flock of those always in need of his services and seldom with the means to pay. He was sympathetic and gentle as he inserted some stitches into my skull. He examined me in those parts where I had been intimately assaulted and said he would contact the Garda, where I was later questioned in a land where such acts are thought better kept out of the public domain, so as not to affect their innocent flock.

Then, from her, who loved and was so close to me as only a mother can, obeyed his rules and told me reluctantly, "Say your prayers and pray to Him who helps all his children."

She gave me a look full of anguish, which said, "Don't blame me. You know how he gets so upset when you don't go to school."

When much later she awoke me with a bowl of hot soup and kissed me as I lay in my bed, the pain didn't seem too bad. My mind was a maelstrom. I could hear my father downstairs shouting, "What in the name of God are we going to do with him? I'm going to find those blackguards who did this to him. I'm going to find out more about this." Exhausted, I slipped back into sleep and dreamland.

It played on my mind so much that I was resolved to tell someone outside my father's zone of stricture. The only person I could think of whom I could trust was the white collared Father who sat in his darkened box and heard all.

There was the holy man sitting behind the mesh. He was the giver of forgiveness, for all who have strayed. His Holy agent, who would listen to all our sins. I sat there waiting my turn, in the usual state of trepidation, to tell him all my most secret thoughts as the shutter was slid aside and then, "Bless me father, for I have sinned."

He listened to my innermost thoughts. When I'd finished telling all except what I really wanted to tell him, he'd murmured, inquiringly, "Was there anything else you wanted to tell me my son?"

Strangely, he seemed to know or sense that something terrible had happened. I was convinced that he knew something. Had the perpetrators confessed? Had my mother been to see him? These wild thoughts flashed through my mind as I hesitated. I was mumbling.

"Speak up. What is it my son?"

"Father, I want to tell you, but it's not easy. I know I must tell someone, or I'll burst with the agony of it."

"What must you tell me, my son?"

Very hesitatingly and mumbling, I said, "I don't know how to say it. It makes me feel so terrible, even thinking about it, but I know I must tell you."

Now, an impatient note in his voice. "Then tell me. You know I'm your spiritual father." Then in the same tone, like a man who has to see lots of other lost souls and, detecting the reluctance and hesitation, sensed my trauma, and said, "Well, come on, my son. We really must try. I'm here to help in all your spiritual matters and give you salvation, from the good Lord above, who gave his life to save our immortal souls. What happened? Where did it happen? When did it happen? I must know if I'm to help you with the Grace of God. We're all here on this earth to help each other and do His work."

With a great effort I began: "When I was fishing, father."

"What happened when you were fishing?"

"There were two men, father."

"What two men child? Please be more specific. Pray tell me. You must not hold anything back, for He knows all."

It was with further great effort that I continued: "They were walking along the riverbank, father, and when they came to where I was fishing, they asked if I'd caught anything as they sat down beside me." I hesitated.

"Go on my child."

"I could tell by the way they spoke that they were from the gypsy camp farther down the river on Maguire's land, who was trying to move them off. The younger of the two, although he had his cap pulled well down over his face, had noticed my school bag and asked if I shouldn't have been at school instead of fishing. I told him that I was excused from school, and he said he didn't believe me and looked into my bag, where he found a half flask of poteen belonging to Jim's father. Jim had left it there. I'd forgotten about it."

The prompting paternal voice, "Go on, my child," and "Yes, my child."

The holy pastor's words cut into my reverie. His voice had the sound of someone who has heard many such tales before. "You have been through a most terrifying ordeal."

I had forgotten for the moment where I was and that someone was listening to my most private thoughts.

He continued: "God will know that you have suffered, and those wicked horrible men will be punished. He knows all. You must realise, my child, that it would not have happened if you'd been in your seat at school. I don't mean by that, that those men are not wicked. As I've said, God will punish them. Now listen carefully and take heed. Try to be a good boy and don't give your parents any extra worry over what they have already. Try and go to school and, although I know that you hate your school, it will not be long before you are leaving, and then you'll have to make your way in the world. That will be like another school, my son, only sometimes much more difficult. Try and pray to the Holy Father, when you are troubled and he will be there to guide you. Now remember what I've told you. Say after me, 'Our Father who art in Heaven, hallowed be Thy name'," and his voice droned on with my voice echoing his words as it has from since I can remember.

An incident so ingrained in a memory, could form an attitude of revulsion in one way and a bizarre curiosity on the other. It was a strange feeling which never left me. It made me hate the very thing I wanted. Would that ever be possible? Does anyone ever get what they want, without a price to pay?

Indelibly printed are such things, which shape you for all your time on this earth.

Later on, there were two men questioned about their movements along the riverbank, where apparently, they had been sighted and were also suspected of stealing some of Maguire's livestock. Evidence had been found at their camp.

The two men fitted the description I had given the Garda and they were released on bail. Later on, there were two naked bodies found in the river far below the falls, near the sea. They had been dealt with, no doubt, by their own kind, who observed certain deep beliefs and moral codes. They would have felt the shame among their group, until it was seen, that they had paid the ultimate price for their grievous crime.

The First Real Queen

And then it happened, my first deeply serious encounter with a mature queen, which was a disaster in quite another way. It seared itself as being such a traumatic bitter sweet episode, after the innocence of a preliminary skirmish from when I wrestled on the riverbank.

When Miss Jennie Croft called at our house, the first thing I remember was her fragrant fresh smell. She was beautiful. I stood close to her as she asked the way to the cottage she would rent. I was very conscious, even then, at the first meeting of the power she could have over me. Was I waiting so fervently for a moment to be truly fulfilled by a regal queen? Fate had decreed that it would only be a matter of time.

I was gazing at her with an effrontery bordering on the impertinent. I kept looking at her, standing there until I was admonished by mother and told to be about my business, but the contact had been made at an early age, which is unlucky for some. She was shapely and so elegantly clad. Why should those sorts of things register forever in an instant? They all combined to instil a sense of queenliness in her and somehow I got the feeling that everything I was thinking should be forbidden, and yet I didn't know why that should be. This reflected earlier admonitions for innocent transgressions. You ask why? Why? Don't ask me. When I would be away from the fields or school, I would go there and peep into her cottage. It was mere deviousness in a craven wish to be near her.

I would look for excuses on one pretext or another to see her. Sometimes I would stop John, our postman, "Hello, John, are there any letters for Miss Croft? I'll take them."

He was pleased because it saved him a longish walk down the lane to where the cottage nestled among the oaks. I didn't know what I might gain, or not gain, except a kind look, even a thank you. Maybe I'd be offered a cup of tea? I just loved to be in her presence. I so wanted to be close to her. I would fantasise about lying at her feet and doing things, just to be pleasing her. Even while she'd look through her letters, or read a paper, I would watch her and she would sometimes look up suddenly and look straight at me and say, "Why do you look at me so?"

I thought she knew all the time why I looked at her, and I could feel my face redden, because she could look through me. Queens can do that. I don't know whether it was a look of kindness or curiosity, the way a mistress might look upon her lap dog.

I often thought, *Why should anyone come and live alone in a cottage?* Wouldn't she be better living in the city with nice handsome men around her? Nobody seemed to come and visit, except the tradespeople. She didn't even seem to go out, except into the garden. She would walk among the many trees in the grounds of the cottage and at times tend the abundant plants and shrubs. At other times she would sit, reading for hours.

Madigan's store delivered everything. I used to watch and sometimes I'd lurk in the bushes and peep through the window at what she would be doing inside. I would watch her move about. What prying? I was a compulsive snoop, or whatever you want to call it. It was always my undoing, as time would tell.

One morning while peering, I couldn't see any movement, so I thought maybe she was in bed and had not yet arisen. I wondered if it were warm in her bed. Was she sleeping, or just lying there?

I wondered at what she was thinking? Was her bed all nice and warm with the sheets all round her body and legs? Thoughts and questions. Would it be warmer if my arms were round her? I blushed deeply at the overpowering thought. Thoughts which were becoming those with knowledge of desire, of possession, and whilst I was thinking thus, there came a touch on my shoulder. I jumped, as a soft female voice asked. "And what do you think you are doing, young lad?"

I jumped again with fright and guilt at beholding who it was. It was none other than her. Guilt was plainly written all over my face, draining of the very blood, and then red with the blushes of embarrassment. Oh, the agony of mangled mental chaos.

I just stood there stammering, "I, er, er, I, I—"

In a stern tone, "Young man, we must talk."

It was more in the nature of a command. It was imperious. Within our relationship she was the one and only prime commander. She was a true queen, commanding her subject. But now I was wrapped in fear and trepidation. I'd been ignominiously caught. The way she looked at me told me that she knew and had complete access to my most private thoughts.

So into the cottage we went, and, motioning to a chair, she said, "Sit down. I'll put the kettle on."

I thought, why go through the ritual of putting the kettle on in my moment of torment. It seemed that everybody put the kettle on in moments of strain or trauma. Some people smoke cigarettes, but most women put the kettle on. She said, "I don't know what you think you're doing, looking in through my windows, but I'm inclined to think the worst and you cannot blame me for thinking so."

When I tried to stutter something, she said, "No, no, no, say nothing and listen to what I'm saying. You see, I came here mostly to get away from people for reasons I needn't explain to you.

I like to be on my own. I like to enjoy my privacy, and I find you peering at me at odd times through bushes, and then peeping through my windows. You make me feel most uncomfortable. I might have to leave here, because this is all something which I never imagined would happen."

The effect of these words gave me a shock and I cried involuntarily, "Oh, no, no, no, you mustn't leave!"

She looked at me, surprised. "Would it upset you very much if I left?"

"Oh, yes, it would, it would. Oh, I should miss you."

"But why should you miss me? I don't know you very well. I've not been here very long. You don't really know me. You're just a very young lad growing up. I'm beginning to think that I don't know you at all. You're a strange boy, and I don't mean that in a bad way. You're very nice in so many ways. But now, I find you creeping through the bushes and peeping through my windows. What am I to think? I don't want to sound like a school ma'am chiding her pupil, you understand. So you see we must talk about this, because there are other matters too."

She continued, "At first I dismissed your antics as boyish enthusiasm. But there's a lot more than that, isn't there? Look at me."

I think so far back, to how lovely she was with her big beautiful blue eyes. As I lie here now the tears come. She was standing over me.

I remember a smell of such sweetness of odours and her eyes had that look that they could know my every thought and she knew it. Why does moisture ensue? Why does it speak for our bodies and our thoughts? I thought about how it speaks in all sorts of ways, from all parts, and the eyes that speak volumes and never say a word. In all our waking lives it's our barometer and will tell the story, awake, sleeping and generated by whatever action or thought that the mind or body may employ, whether emotional or physical because the eyes are the conduit to everything. I felt a reactive nervous response to her every utterance affecting all my wants and desires.

And so it was there, that as the tears welled up in my shame, that she put her arms around me in a motherly sort of way, without the slightest suggestion of anything but a maternal reaction and said in a low voice, the way she would speak to a handicapped child, and surely that is really what I was, "You are so young, so very young, and just into your teens. You're beginning your life. When I say to you that I want to be alone it doesn't mean that I don't like you. You're probably lonely too, just the same as me. We're at a crossroads. Our ages can make it impossible for us to be close in some ways and yet not so very much apart. Do you understand what I mean?"

I had mumbled something incoherently as she concluded, "You see, we've been fashioned in different moulds and convention makes us act so."

She still had her arm around me all through saying this. My arms went around her as a reaction, as I laid my head against her bosom. She was much taller than I.

I was listening and hanging on every word she was saying. Although, in a way I was being scolded, I was being transported. Just her holding me close, a small statue in dimension, reciprocating. Some moments may only come on that level, once in a lifetime. It's the mental and not the physical, the love returned, the succouring harbour so close to lie against, like bodies fusing into each other.

As we stood there, my thoughts were rampant. It was like being in a miraculous maternal embrace of sorts, but not quite. There was more to it than that. I didn't care and I held onto this lovely creature that was all mine for that very brief moment. No turning back for me now, not ever, from this queen. No spurning. I looked up into her face, which was blushing in the most enchanted way. She said, "Now look at me. Aren't I the silly person? That kettle will be boiling. I'll make the tea."

If that had been now, much later in my life, I should have shouted, *For God's sake, what are you worrying about tea for? There are more important matters pending.*

My vocabulary existed in another time-scale, so I meekly say, "Yes of course."

As I sat down, looking at the floor and thinking of nothing, you think of everything and you listen to the bustle of the teacups and the saucers and the spoons and you wonder why, not knowing at this time what was in store, what magic moments which might come into my life. Joyous or agonising, the price I would have to pay, unbelievable at times, for joys indescribable, and in the world of their strictures, forbidden. The price is always exacted. The price exacted in *exactium*, *exactimorium*, *exactantus* and tea being poured. There's always something pouring. Pouring from, pouring into, pouring out, and pouring down.

"You'll feel better when you've had this cup of tea. Don't be too upset. I may have chided you a little but I care and we must not go around peering or prying. Remember what I've said, won't you?" she said, looking at me as if interrupting my thoughts, "and we'll forget about this silly little episode."

She didn't quite convince me, as I mumbled something, but she knew by the look on my face and in my eyes that the last thing I would do, would be to forget about her. She had cast her spell and it was indestructible. Nothing could stifle it. It would grow, despite any attempt to abort it or try to stop it, destroy it, kill it, terminate it or otherwise. Seeds of such indestructibility sown into the young embryo of a baby's heart would be unstoppable. Looking into her eyes without my saying anything other than murmuring,

"Oh, yes, yes," she knew, too, that the seed would grow into a strangle grip on my very being. She read my thoughts and there was a look of futility written on her lovely face. But there was hope written there too and I could read that. But no, no more tears.

"Why aren't you drinking your tea?"

I thought, for **** sake, this cup of bloody tea. Later, when the tea had been drunk and gone, she had regained her composure and I was no longer required. I got the feeling that in polite fashion I had been dealt with and was being dispensed with for now. Nothing so much as, "now remember our little chat," or, "I'll maybe see you tomorrow or later." There was just nothing. Didn't she realise I had been fully activated and I was not expecting a few curt nods of dismissal, or expecting to be discarded? Will those regal Queens ever realise the damage they can do, when propounding from their pedestals?

"Now take care, dear Mal, and be a good boy. Bye."

My head was full of thoughts as I made my way along the lane and kicked the loose pebbles and likened myself to no more than a tiny pebble on a constantly changing seashore, being tossed hither and tither by the waves of human emotions, forever in the eons of time.

In the sanctuary of my room, I lay and tried to find answers to all those questions which teemed in a confused enquiring mind, until there was solace in sleep, but never without the dreams.

While thinking about her, I was determined that I was going to act like a man, a real man. I was on the threshold, and I was going to make that step from boy to man. And yet, there were so many questions left unanswered. Draw down the blind and block out the puzzling haze.

The next morning, everything looked much brighter with the new day. With a child's anticipation I went to meet the Postman.

"Hello, John. Are there any letters for Miss Croft?"

He said, "Yes, yes. I suppose you want to take them, Mal."

"Yes, I'm going that way. I'll drop them in for you, save you walking that stretch of the lane."

He smiled with a friendly wink as he gave me the letters. His smile was the smile of a man who had walked many miles over many years, delivering dreams in letters. He had amassed a gentle wisdom, much more than many philosophers on the feelings hidden deep in letters from young hearts.

And I knocked on the cottage door with joy and some trepidation.

The door opened and she was smiling as she looked at me quizzically.

"Good morning, young Mal." She noticed the letters held in my hand. "Thank you for bringing my letters. I'm sure John is pleased with your services."

She was half laughing as she was saying this with a whimsical smile. She knew all my thoughts. She was reading me like a printout. But to me, it was like a greeting from Cleopatra to Caesar. She was looking so beautiful and regal, like a goddess who could never have been touched. All those silly things which can go through a mind at such a pace, and I'm mumbling, "Yes, I'm all right, thank you." I don't know what possessed me as I said, "Do you think I could have some tea, please?" I mean, that surprised me. It was bravery born of desperation. Amazingly, she didn't seem to be taken aback, or even look surprised at my request.

"Ah, you'd like a cup of tea. Well of course. Come along, I was just about to put the kettle on."

She looked briefly at the handwriting on the letters and left them on the small table. I could see she hadn't long been arisen from her bed. She had the queenly dressing-gown look. That's what made her look so regal. One of those gowns which clung to her body. As I watched her walk away I thought of yesterday when she had put her arms around me. Is there any excuse, I can think of, to make her put them around me again, even in maternal fashion?

I was amazed at my thoughts.

I said, "Is there anything I can help you with?"

"Yes, you can fill the kettle."

She was so in charge, living in her little kingdom, and me so servile. She said, "Did you want to talk to me about anything special?"

I stuttered, "Er, what do you mean?"

"Don't mumble," she said. "You obviously want to see me, otherwise you wouldn't ask the postman to give you my letters."

Oh, she knew all about that too, did she? My face was colouring up.

"Oh, oh, yes, well, well, er, er—"

She interrupted me again. "You're here and you're seeing me and you're pleased with what you see?"

"Ye-yes, yes," I stammered. This had taken me aback. She always had the upper hand.

"Well," she said, "I'm glad you've come. I'm pleased to see you. You don't have to look at me through the bushes or snoop. You can just come and visit me like an ordinary person. How is that? You may knock on my door and say you'd like to come in and see me if I'm here, but I don't want you to go round crawling and peeping."

I was so surprised and thrilled by what she said, which meant so much.

"You mean I can come and visit you if I want to and sit and talk with you?"

"Yes. That is as long as you don't have any other chores to do or your parents don't mind, you can come and talk, but you'll never say anything very much if you only mumble and answer with more mumbles. I don't think you understand yourself very much. You're so introspective, but you are a nice boy and I like you. You must stop looking in at yourself, look out more.

I have a feeling that you always look in at windows to see what the world is doing. I know mine are not the only windows you have looked into. Even when you're on your bicycle you look into other people's windows, I know. People know you ride slowly past and stop and peer into their private lives, so to speak. Maybe it's only an inquisitive young boy's curiosity. There's no harm in that. Maybe there's something more to it, eh? I don't think some people mind, but it can make some feel uncomfortable when they happen to look out and there you are staring in at them."

I can feel my face so red. I was being chided and played with, perhaps a mere toy for the cynical amusement of someone who was probably bored and enjoyed analysing this curious boy. Somehow she had heard about my cycling and looking in at windows.

I blurted, "You're making fun of me—"

She cut in, "You must be prepared for that if you're going to come and visit me any time you wish. We shall have to talk and engage in all kinds of conversation. You must give as well as you receive, as good as you get, but answer properly, or I will have to put you on a leash and call you my pet dog, and if you don't even bark I'll have to give you a name."

I laughed a little at this. I didn't mind being the object, although I wasn't pleased at how lowly I'd been levelled. *How lucky the dog*, I thought.

Perhaps he could be at the foot of the bed or on the bed. Without thinking, I said, "Being a pet could be nice."

A smile flickered and broke all over her beautiful face.

"I can see we are not without perception. So you think that a pet might have some privileges which, no doubt, you might enjoy." I was cornered and an answer had to be given.

"I meant, er, yes, like he could have, er ..." and I blushed. Of course, she read me like a book. This queen understood my mind to such a degree of accuracy that I felt denuded of all private thoughts, which made my situation worse. I resolved there at that time not to think any thoughts other than that which she might like. I must think nothing about her legs any more or any part of her, or the shape of her, when she leaned over to pour the tea. I mustn't think these things. She seemed to know all.

She said, "Don't feel uncomfortable. Your thoughts are most natural for one growing into manhood. You are but a very young plant that's about to blossom. Plants sometimes blossom better when tended a little. Sometimes they need help."

She said it in such a way that it seemed to me like she understood it all. She knew the whole way of it.

She continued, "We must get onto more light-hearted things and discuss other matters."

Just like that, she could switch me on, and then switch me off with one sentence, and she asked, "What do you plan to do today?"

"Cecil and I will go to the fields."

"I see. You really like being with your four-legged friend. You don't like school much, do you?"

"I'm not going to school any more to be hurt by their canes and straps."

She smiled, in her wicked lovely way. "You must go. I mean, you'll be a young man soon. You could take an interest in biology. Do you like nature studies?"

Again, that lovely wicked smile. Then she laughed at some private joke.

I could only mumble, "Er, yes I am, a little."

"Ah, yes," she said, "the birds and the bees, yes. Well think of yourself growing up. Think of yourself as a suitable object for biological study. What applies to all the other little creatures, applies to you and me in exactly the same way." This was probably the first practical lesson I'd ever experienced. She'd made her point, and I was just a little too young to grasp the whole impact, but not too young to grasp how it seemed to take a weight off my shoulders, due to not having realised until that moment that unconsciously I was feeling guilty about something, but not quite sure or able to make out what it was. As I sat there she said other things and I listened to her lovely voice flow on, and I was still thinking about all creatures, following their instincts and who eventually achieve their life-propagating function.

She watched my expression and said, "Ah, you're deep in thought again. Now we're looking in again, aren't we? Why such introspection? What are you thinking now?"

"Oh," I said, "I wasn't thinking about anything in particular." I lied.

"You are always thinking about something, but one thing at a time. It's only natural that you will do so, until you climb to the top of your mountain. But first of all, we've got to get rid of this dreadful shyness if we are going to be real friends, for there is no need to be shy with me. Come over here."

It was another imperious command, and I stood up meekly as she led me to the bedroom and to the bed. "Sit down."

What commands, what commands from this queen. Enthralling. "Do you like my bed?"

"Oh, yes, yes."

"I knew you'd like it. You'd like it better if we were inside, wouldn't you?"

Such words nigh overwhelmed me as I stuttered, "Er, er," I just did not know what to say in reply. But I wanted very much to shout out loud, "Yes, Yes."

"Remember," she said, "we had a nice hug yesterday and we were both very happy to be close."

She laughed now. Her laughter made me delighted. I was transported. "I'm going to hug you again," she said, "but in a different way." She turned round to embrace me and kiss me in a way I never knew was possible. So different to the way my mother and my aunts had kissed me and even Molly. My body was electric. Many things were happening to it, which I didn't know were possible. Great surging was taking place. Extraordinary movements were happening in my lower anatomy. A feeling of strength combined with surging, seeking fulfilment. Toppling over the precipice as I involuntarily erupted. I blurted out, as if she knew, and she did, "Oh, I'm sorry."

Why, did I say that? I don't know. How could she know, but she did. She wouldn't know what happened completely, maybe, but she looked at me and she knew and she laughed, wickedly, though she wasn't wicked. But I knew as she laughed and laughed, that she would always laugh at me. The queen laughs at her subject. The queen summons her subject. The queen dismisses her subject.

"Ah," she said, "ha, ha. We have erupted, have we not? Are you uncomfortable?" She kept quietly laughing and I could have cried. Such joy mixed with a little humiliation reflecting my inexperience of such bodily emotional expression. It was much more convulsing than when I was with Molly.

She teased, "Should I hug and kiss you again or give you one of my special hugs. It seemed to have an agreeable effect on you."

She knows all the while that I am trying to settle myself in my wetness, mumbling incoherently against her light-hearted bantering laughter. And then, "Young man, I've got things to do now. I'll see you again soon. Bye for now."

I was being dismissed, thrown aside like a child would a toy, with which she had become bored. To be deflated so quickly from heavenly bliss one minute, and then to feel so desolate and dismissed the next and all accompanied by her impish laughter. Could it all be just a pleasant amusing distraction to a bored lovely lady who knows the ways of the world?

She ushered me to the door, and said, "Don't forget to bring my letters, young Mal. Bye."

She was still smiling curiously at me as her door closed.

I brooded on this for days. How could I free myself from the compulsion of a craving to be even laughed at some more if it meant being close to her? She already had such a sway over me, and it was as if I were inextricably drawn to the cottage and her.

As I sat upon Cecil on our way to the fields, he was the only one I could tell about it.

So it was, that some days later, I knocked on her door in trepidation, anticipation, but with determination.

"So you're back, young lad, with the post. What a gallant little postman you are."

I said, "There are no letters. I just wanted to see you."

"Well, you had better come in then."

"Thank you." I sat there in desperation, things so strong within me that would overcome all obstacles. She smiled as she went about her task, the ritual of making tea. I was in torment and conflict with her and myself, and yet intrigued and delighted to be enslaved.

Why did I think about the moral advice from the Holy Father, sitting in his dark box behind the grill? Why am I feeling so guilty in my blind craving to be so close with her?

In desperation I mutter, "May I have another hug?" I blurt out, "I just want to hold you, I don't want tea."

To my astonishment she didn't seem the least surprised at my outburst.

"If you really want to hug me, of course you can." And leaning over, she kissed me like that again, but it didn't happen this time, although it nearly did, and I knew if she touched me it would. How could I get through this barrier? When I think about it, it all seems so crazy, so inevitable, and so stupid. I was the little mouse being toyed with by the cat, before the final act. She seemed to know exactly every emotion I went through and when she kissed me again she whispered, "You like that, don't you? You're very determined.

You've made your mind up to go through with it, haven't you?"

She took care of the whole thing. It could be considered as the initiation of a child's maturing body, to be put to its proper function. What would I find in the end? Would I be happier? Fulfilled? Looking for that realisation of something, whatever it was. It could be likened to the suicidal lemmings going out to sea. I had to be eaten, killed, crushed and hurt and suffer the experience—the joyful agony of being eventually over fulfilled and yet unfulfilled.

If she only knew what I was going through. No answers are capable of knowing what had been endured in this so young and as yet untried body. Would it ever realise its dream and the realisation that it craved?

Dream on, dream on. Can it possibly be? It's all for the best or the worst and the knowledge of today, coming from the frustrations of yesterday. Who can answer? Too young to know the sadness of total disownment, as was my case afterwards, and a mother, once so close, who told them that they should confine me for my own good if they thought it was best for me.

And now there is a day of watery green, no pearl of emotion, no touching with the hand that was once so warm and full of promise. It wasn't always cold. Who could ever imagine such a feeling as I experienced the intense sensual heat of her cleaving as she finally unfolded her mystery to ease my craving, to be forever seared into an enduring total first experience.

Afterwards, when the queen bee had discarded her aspiring plaything, it caused the empty depressive days of deflation. Such a crushing sadness, as the succouring haven was abruptly closed to my immature hungering for love. It seemed that I would always be in never-ending despair.

It was the void of total emptiness of not seeing her and the vacuum of loving suction, existing in a body of malfunction, creating evermore introspectiveness that would endure within a craven lost soul.

Did I ascend to descend? Was the summit ever to be reached? Did I feel better for being the recipient of those heavenly moments at her shrine? Was I worthy of being there at all, under the queenly command of her who wished to be amused or thrilled by someone who had temporarily assuaged her inner vicarious appetites?

Stop thinking so much and be quiet. You search for too many answers, because your torment disables your ability to cope. You'll never cope. Why didn't you just savour and enjoy the experience, without all the complications. Don't be the idiot who is only capable of bad semaphore and mumbling, so wanting to cling to the moment forever and would die in the attempt if necessary? How could you ever hope to cope with such a queen? You were never in command.

Too many thoughts surge through a young mind ill-equipped to understand. Just enjoy the moment. Why didn't you do that?

The desires of the very young, are so strong in their blind quest. When in her queenly presence, she could do things with me, as she enjoyed my weird and bizarre fulfilment, by being amused at my very malfunctions.

In any event, I was in my own special heaven when she utterly controlled her plaything. To be commanded by her so completely, to enjoy her usage of me. It was what I craved. Wasn't it fantastic for me? No cold back to be turned on the child seeking love. But why the critical word, when a kind one could have saved me and spared me the utter despair.

The institutions are crammed full of those who didn't pass her examination, and didn't live up to her norm, and you are definitely on that list. When they arrive in their white coats, don't make a fuss. It can be very upsetting. Go quietly, because you'll need the quiet and rest and certainly you'll receive their caring treatment.

These kind people will look after you always. That phrase, "look after you," as they do look after you mostly, but within their rules, having taken into consideration the combination of events that combine to make one into a first class candidate. You just can't say, "Look it's not my fault. If I hadn't been seduced by her queenliness, I wouldn't be like this. I wouldn't be in this state.

If she hadn't been making game with me, this wouldn't have happened." They don't want to hear all that, they regard that as the ramblings of an unstable mind.

But in reality, it wasn't as straightforward as that, and she didn't seduce her plaything immediately. She played about with me for those summer months and mentally nearly killed me with her fiendish acts as she sought new avenues to explore. She really enjoyed being able to make me wet at her command.

This craving madness probably did drive me mad. All the time, I was absolutely consumed with the one thought and all the delayed action wasn't helping and whatever thoughts I might have had, was for her to exploit me in the fulfilment of her weird desires and wishes.

Of course, I wanted her to use me as her plaything to be seduced forever. I know it's my entire fault. Did I not always want to be crucified by some queenly body? Why wasn't she just another sensual woman who grabbed me and evacuated my seeking, which at least, would have been honest? It would all have been so much better, and then to have left it at that? Why didn't they listen when I tried to explain it all to them?

Can I give them a name, an address, and say, "Go on, go and see her. She's the cause of all this, she's responsible. Put the blame on her. Go on, ask her why she kept making me wet my trousers?"

Those demeaning acts were adroitly aimed at inadequacies of the already lost soul.

Eventually her hands touched me in my very private area, and I went through the excruciating pain and joy of such joys as I experienced the climax of all that seeking. But what might I have been capable of, given a more loving, kindly approach? All I craved was the right word of encouragement. A little of herself, perhaps. Just give me a tiny bit of confidence. Oh please, just give me the assurance and succour I craved.

It was all about being truly wanted, really loved. When you are told you are wanted and loved, even an idiot like me could have been brim-full of confidence, gratefulness and adoration of such a kindly queen.

Why does a young mind imagine that it could all come true? As you learn and know in the fullness of time, nothing can be sustained at such a peak.

Who would believe it, if I told them about the day when she'd finally decided to fulfil her mouse? She would bring to the surface, the most intimate parts of my body to be inspected, observed at length by her, and her sweet voice telling me that she was going to satisfy me, and I, in desperate innocence, believed her.

Looking at me she said, "Oh, my dear Mal, so young, and we haven't got very much to start with, but I have a feeling, that we will manage." All this while gazing at me with her most queenly reassuring smile. She continued as she veritably purred, whispering, "We'll make it greatly improve."

I believed everything she said. What comparisons could I make? She was the authority. So when it happened, I began to worry about the whole thing so desperately. It set my biological clock back forever, and I could not face her gender for many years after this experience. I'm still mindful of the fact that I had brought it on myself. I was the one caught snooping, remember? I was the one looking through the window. She didn't ask me to come snooping, she didn't ask me to waylay the postman and deliver her letters. She didn't ask me to do anything at all. When you think about it, was I not the prime mover?

Had many others graduated at her alter before me? Was that the real cause of those tears in her eyes when it finally happened? Didn't she realise what she had done? The tears, they never failed. Her face and the tears enslaved me. But all I craved was a tear of love. I would have done it all over again for that fractional, most precious moment of closeness with her arms round me. Could it ever possibly end in real fulfilment? The crazy thing is, if she came here today, I'd still be a bubbling mass of subservience to any wish she might have, no matter what. She would have that effect on me. I would just dissolve before her and pray for her command. *Open your trousers, boy. Ah, yes, have a look. It's improving. Why are you blushing?*

Could the dominant role be ever mine?

No, I never wanted the dominate role. It was to be avoided, because that would have made me responsible. Responsible? A role for queens to play who can dictate the way their realm, their body, will be used. No question or doubt about it, to be manipulated in such a fashion, not knowing at what points the strings would be pulled, for the puppet to play his role. Then the final culmination, when it happened and our bodies fused and I so deeply entwined within her, blending our fluids for that climactic first time. My craving body seemed to gush and gush. She had it all planned, in every detail. I know that now. To tell myself that I made the running when I was snooping, now seems fanciful. She could have so easily told this stupid boy to be about his business, but she didn't, because she could see some harmless fun to be had with someone so naive, so innocently seeking.

She had dictated and conducted the whole enterprise, step by step. It was her sense of fun, when my guided hand was allowed to go into her queenliness. A queenly body so malleable and moulded so perfectly, as if especially just for me. She would get a buzz every time she knew I had wetted when I touched her as directed.

She could be so many different persons, at different times, but it was always her, just to adore and serve.

Why did she get me into such a mental state that I couldn't put those blocks together?

Those blocks really punished me. They were mocking me in the shapes I made with them. Ha, ha, a suitable case indeed. Yes, you'll be all right. Yes, we'll look after you very well. And when I lay under the bed, that was a happy time, because I wasn't observed and they could never understand what I meant by lying under. I always enjoyed lying under because I was the secret interloper, the hidden trespasser, and I shouldn't have been there. The learned man in the field of pursuing his analysis associated it with repressed desires in a subconscious. So I'd heard and I'd listened and I'd eavesdropped and I'd conjured up all my pictures of what really happened. Was it on the surface or beneath? Was I beneath when I'd failed?

Why did I sneer to myself at the big Father of His Flock enveloped in the cloth of his calling when I eavesdropped on his tryst? At least he had made a better fist of it then me. At least he seemed to be reconciled to his lot. Why should I be critical? Certainly not from practical experience, and it was something he had accepted with a mature purpose, and he was right. To him, it was purely a bodily function and he accepted that, although his vows forbade it.

I shouldn't have listened. I shouldn't have been under the bed. I should have said, "Look here, I'm under this bed, and you can't have a relationship on it. I don't mean you're wrong to have a relationship, but I mean I shouldn't be here, I'm a third party. I've no part in this f**k.

I've no part in any of the proceedings at all and then the other man who wore the white collar of his calling, might have shouted back to me, "You're so right my son and so considerate, so please, would you just **** off yourself, as we only have a short time in which to complete this **** and we don't have any time to waste, so please would you go. There's a good lad, run along about your business." And me, being just another child of his flock, would have gone and left them to it.

Well, it's no good thinking about that because I didn't say it. I didn't tell them I was there under the bed and that's that. All I knew was that our mother had giggled and groaned and frolicked with our pastor. Maybe his resounding fart after finishing was the only thing to remember about the whole episode. Perhaps that could be all that mattered. A cloud of very holy gaseous air, by way of a blessing on the whole affair. It may very well have been the most important discharge in the whole proceedings.

Thinking back to the queen on that day when I had fulfilled her purpose, she decided she would spoil her object of fun, so besotted and dedicated to her every wish. Was it not ridiculous? The putty to be moulded into her plaything, teasing, tantalising, touching, for her bit of fun. Then it happened and once again, after my premature wetness, when she coaxed me on and caressed my body as no other could, she said, "This is the last of the blood-letting.

You're going to be so manly in your love today, because today you're going to be my king."

I couldn't say anything. I was just heaving all the time and my frame was shuddering. I looked at her and I could forgive her anything. She was so serene and queenly. She could wear her lovely smile and melt me and make me go all silly again. "Now come along. This is going to be your victory. Today you'll reach the summit of all your yearning." She was in charge of everything. She poured some sweet-tasting amber liquid into two glasses, which was warming and lovely to drink. Not a bit like Ginger's poteen. After a few minutes, the effect was electric, and I was full of control and confidence.

I felt secure and, for the very first time, I was in charge and confident in spite of all her self-indulgence at my expense, as her off-beat enjoyments were all cast aside, and I was drawing so very close to her queenly flesh. So close that this time it must happen. She led me into her bedroom, and we sat on her bed. She poured another glass. Then she slipped off her silk dressing gown and let it fall. She took my hand and, thrusting it deep between her queenly thighs, said, "You can put it where you like." I shuddered in a painful joy of anticipation as she whispered, "Come on, you know where I want you to put it."

Of course I knew. I so wanted to put it there. I made a hurried move and she firmly gripped my hand and thrust it deeper and tighter, and I was in such trembling. She held it so tightly between her strong limbs, that it would suffocate me with the sensation of it all. "Now what's all this? Don't you want to love me?" And she kissed me and kissed me again and now I was on my way, the lemming, which nothing could stop, not even death itself. I was enslaved in my desire, as I was coming to fruition and again and again, and all that wanting, all that struggling, thrusting. She was moaning, "Take it easy, and take it easy."

I wasn't hearing. I was crashing on. I was there. I was there. I was so deep inside my queen. I was there, evacuating my very heaving body and soul into her queenliness. It was the most magical experience. It was the most heavenly journey of seeking. It was the end of the world amid the stars, as she allowed me to be so encased within her regal flesh. To experience such heavenly emotion in the very core of my being and being allowed to supplicate and adore, seemingly forever at that moment, when we were as one. She had never given so much before.

At last, I had been allowed to be her king. She had opened her pent up appetites and given vent to the free expression of her body and soul. The overburdened udder had never been milked so utterly, and why did she decide to allow total access anyway? What had changed her mind? Why did she decide to start me off at all? What was in that magical drink that had removed all constraints?

Such fulfilment and fulfilling upheaval at being inside her was a flowery field full of early morning dewy wetness, the scent of her roses mixed with the perfumed smell of steamy musky flesh, of pure heavenly bliss. Was this or could this be? Was it all real? Her hands were guiding and teaching. All succouring and nothing imposed. And I was speeding again and again, discharging into the most delectable gooey messy mix of each other.

It was all so glorious in all the assurance of a craving so fulfilled. Could such a queen ever be deemed carnal or impure? Had I at last found a harbour of safety, a safe secure heavenly place to berth? To be allowed in all her most private crevices of no light and yet, sublime enlightenment? Maybe answers don't come out of crevices. Maybe those harbours of safety are harbours of enslavement, with a continual hungering to achieve again and again, but wondering somehow if such a wondrous experience could ever be repeated in the same way.

It had to happen, in that events subsequently caused me to slip into days of depression and introspection in the realisation of a pup's foolishness. I can't tell them all of this because they won't listen. They would think I was really nuts. My big sin in their eyes is the non-contribution to their society. They call it withdrawal, a great passiveness, complete dereliction, failing according to their rules, to make the required contribution to a society, which I was never at one with.

The queen could have explained it to them. She could have told them how it all happened between us. She could have explained it all.

All these thoughts fly by seemingly in a fraction of a second and yet they are stored so indelibly in memory and still they can be wondrously graphic as I strive to recapture the magical moments which sowed the imagery and emotion forever in a mind that seeks solace in the very pain of recapturing times past.

Aftermath

Then it all came to an end, and the first impressions always being the deepest, became a form of preoccupation with the promised splendour that was never to be repeated again. It left its mark and set the pace for the rest of time in my reaction to those who would come close ever after.

The queens of this world should hold up their signs and say, "Enter and Exit at our pleasure, or even at your peril." It can be like a cul-de-sac in the mind, from which there is no exit.

In human life, there are always the casebook notes which have been made on the various segments, happenings, so formed by an unforgettable experience. I agonised as I watched a despairing mother who could never quite know what ailed or shaped her son to make him thus.

When I would look at her face, once so beautiful and so young, and look into her mind, I could hear her thoughts. *Why is he so odd? All we need from him is a little co-operation. It's for your own good. We're only trying to help you.*

What's happened to you lately? You've changed so completely in the last six months.

Why always their questions? I couldn't truly answer and was somewhat ashamed when they asked for answers which would expose my innermost thoughts and desires that I had always been told were sinful and not good for me.

The inquisitorial seeking of answers from me would never solve the problem. The puzzle is me, a suitable case. I repeat, I couldn't possible tell them my innermost cravings and therefore could never ever explain myself to them.

And then Cecil began ailing. I hadn't been able to spend much time with him, because they now had him working hard all day. Father had cruelly hired him out to the brewery with their heavily laden drays. It was too much of a strain for Cecil, who could pull a plough, but not those drays over the cobbled streets for twelve-hour shifts.

Needless to recount, he began to fail and they couldn't understand it. When he was returned to his stable, I lay beside his big exhausted frame in the evenings as he rested from his labours with badly shod hoofs that were used to fields and turf.

I could have told them that all he wanted was kindness and a lesser burden so he could cope. The vet man said his big heart was failing and there was nothing for it but to let him live out his time in pasture and love. After all, he was now becoming long past his prime. Had he not done his fair share of work in his lifetime?

I made my usual visit to his stable early one morning as usual, to make sure he was fed and watered ready for his day of toil. Then came the dreaded moment. Instead of greeting me, he just lay in his stall. So I lay down beside him. He laid his head on my chest as he gave me a last tearful look. Soon after, his honest, kindly soul departed, and he never moved again. Needless to say, I was desolate and, to top it all, it was the same day that Miss Jennie Croft, my queen of love, had dismissed me in the coldest, cruellest terms. Even now, I want to die when I think about it.

Dismissal

She had said in her most imperious tone, when I was looking for sympathy and telling her about Cecil, "I don't care about your Cecil. It's just another animal, and I don't want you to visit me again, Mal. Don't come to see me ever again. Don't come to the cottage. I don't want to see you again. You're all mixed up."

I was stunned. What could I say? I couldn't speak. Do you just mumble and say, "I adore you, please, oh please, don't be so cruel. Don't break my heart."

I'm thinking, no more ecstatic pain, no more the piece of putty to be moulded, and I pleaded, "Don't send me away. Can't there be even a last time?" As I'm saying this, I feel that my heart will never stand the strain of losing Cecil and my queen. The two most important beings in my life taken away from me in the same day. I just could not cope.

"You may kiss me, but it's the last time."

That was when I bit her. She should never have asked me to put my head there again, to keep kissing her deep among those parts, as I had done in the past, just to please her. It must have hurt a lot, as I sank my teeth into her other extended lips in her most private place. She screamed and laughed and pulled my head by the hair and struck me on the face, as I knew that I would forever feel the taste of her wet musky flesh.

In times past, when the teacher's voice broke into my reverie, when the taste of her flesh still lingered in my mouth, and my mind was miles away in another world, I would be so preoccupied when the stern Christian Brothers' voice broke into my most private thoughts. "Wake up there, boy. You must concentrate. I'll repeat the question." Always questions, always.

"I didn't hear you, sir." In my mind I'd think of her and say to myself, *You see the trouble you're getting me into? I'm always thinking about you.* More questions, no answers.

I couldn't keep away. After school, I walked along the usual path down the lane and through the trees, and I saw John Carroll's big removal lorry make its way along the lane. With an involuntary shudder of shock, I knew it could only be going to one place and I kept walking, just to convince myself that it was good-bye. I stood a little distance and watched the progress of the moving men as they carried the contents of the cottage and carefully stored them inside the truck.

It was all very impersonal to them, doing a job, which they had done so many times, with clinical detachment as being just another day's work. Just another job to them, you might say, but to me, it was the final wrench, especially as I watched her bed and the little bedside table being packed away. They could never know the complete fulfilment of all my yearning, which I had known between its sheets, with a magical queenly tutor, who seared a love tryst that would forever be with me.

There was no sign of her and I knew with a pang, that she would have been driven to the station much earlier, in case I should show up, and she was right. Why go through all that again?

As my tears quietly flowed, I realised she had made her decision. She realised the implications of her actions and the inevitable consequences that would follow if they were to continue, in that what to her was a vicarious sensual experiment with a confused young soul, would forever influence a young mind in all matters relating to her gender, and she would return to a society from whence she had sought solace from a previous unhappy relationship.

I would relive our last moments together. I just could not get rid of this deep preoccupation, which was causing more and more problems, and I had become dilatory and was unable to concentrate on anything. I would continually put my tongue around my lips remembering the taste of her moist flesh.

I kept thinking about Cecil. Who else could I tell my most private thoughts to? Who else could I tell my troubles to? That lovable, kindly beast of toil had been my last sheet anchor.

Now, all things in which I had formerly taken some interest are being neglected in the cold, cold light of yesterday as I cry out the question, *Why? Why?*

Winter comes and empty are the rooms of receptiveness. No point in my seeking reasons. Go on, carry your emptiness with you. No more meeting, no wetting, no queenly juices, gone forever. Now I find flaws when I pick the red rose from your garden, and you, the loveliest, most regal, the irrigator of the plants, projected into my life, have gone back to a place from whence you had thought to escape from your own mistakes and try to forget, and then I happened and you knew that was a big mistake and a grievous sin.

It was frightening. No queen, no Cecil. It couldn't go on, and I knew they would come for me again with their puzzles and their blocks. Why ask me how quickly could I get the blocks in order? Another intelligence test to assess and go through the maze. All sorts of clever people would assess me.

Such people had been born on farms of hard-working parents, struggling to keep their small farms going. But those parents were prepared to make any sacrifice so their sons and daughters could go to higher places of learning and wouldn't have to plough the hard stony ground, nor weed the drills, nor thin the mangle, so that when they finished at their seat of learning and had passed their exams, would then be qualified to go among us and give us the benefit of their now trained minds, now presumably qualified to test my processes, my capability, my function. Needless to say, I couldn't solve their simple testing puzzles or put their blocks in the right order, in any order. All I could think of was Cecil and the queen, now gone forever.

Sarah and Molly had gone to England to join that most noble nursing profession, giving succour to the sick and ailing in John Bull's Land, while Britain was involved in the titanic struggle of World War II.

Why couldn't I do that stupid puzzle? Why couldn't I give them the correct answers to their simple questions? I had never been good at answers, so they decided that I was a case worthy of attention and they'd take good care of me as ever.

The Cycling Window
Looking Phase

I had started cycling again. During my cycling period, I enjoyed the challenge of pushing against a headwind, the rain trying to penetrate through my old waterproof jacket. I would be hot with the exertion of it all.

That could possibly have been my best and most perceptive period, whilst moving through a landscape of people's lives as they were surveyed by me and my pedals. It was the intriguing windows and their shutters registering a Georgian era in a once grand city, all part of a grander empire.

From such an early age, it was always accepted that, in their ethos of the sacred church of the white collar and black smock, our most Holy Fathers got their message across. They preached, and I was in no doubt that, as far as they were concerned, all sex for pleasure was a sin and a criminal offence against Him. Except in the propagation of your own kind in the holy state of matrimony through the love of a good woman with whom you had gone through their ritual, made it legal in the eyes of Him to produce more of His flock for our wellbeing and support of our pastors. What a paradox.

According to them, a woman should never hold you, unless "They" had said you were licensed to do so, because you had gone through their patented contract, which bound you to a lifetime doing it and making lots more of your kind to fill their seats of worship and keeping them in business.

My thoughts, my pastor had said during a confessing of my sins in his darkened box, were unhealthy. He said that I was far too young to be even thinking about such things. I was to concentrate when at school and do lots of hard work to help my worried parents.

Yes, that was the antidote. Hard work was the key, and the young pup to be purged of blasphemy and wanton lust. He of the Cloth was a good man of honesty and integrity, as had been taught him in that place where they ordain them in this world to prepare us for the next. He gave what he thought was a lot of good advice and instilled a certain aura of fear—terrible punishments to come in the fire-filled furnace if we didn't conform to His teachings.

He had totally bemused me when he used phrases like "in the fear and love of God," and I thought greatly how could I love someone and fear them at the same time.

My Mother said I had to visit him on regular occasions, to expunge my soul of all its sins and unworthiness and tell him of my bodily bad habits. Be utterly repentant, so that he may grant me his most Holy Absolution.

After my encounter with the queen I just could not face him at all. This caused a lot of trouble with her of the cold back, who absolutely despaired of the loss of my soul and said this was all the cause of my later trouble. The Pastor said to me on one occasion, while kneeling in his box, "Understand, my son, that we must resist all desires that waste the seed of our Lord."

A Fathers Dalliance and the Doc

And then when our sire, the prodigal father, returned, having being spurned after a cold winter by his new and so-young queen, our hard-toiling mother forgave him and once again he ruled.

Now to justify her forgiveness, he had to take more interest in his worrying off-spring, which is where we come to the dog.

In most persons lives there is a dog. Our sire now fancied himself as a man of field sports. Any wild animal, minding its own business, could be deemed fair game. Came one day when he piled everything and everyone into his old Hillman gate change car, which required starting with a lot of cranking. When it spluttered into life, he would make for the Dublin Hills, where many unsuspecting rabbits and other wildlife who wished to be left in peace, had their lives disrupted. And so one Sunday morning, it was off into the great uncharted.

His had bought from a man in a pub, what he was told, was the perfect retriever. Not being the very best shot, he had been through a few dogs, none of which had quite fitted the bill. His latest acquisition sounded promising and not a moment to be lost to see him in action.

The man, who'd sold him the dog while they consumed a fair quantity of the black stuff, had said that he was a brilliant retriever and our sire was getting a real bargain. On the day in question, we arrived at a likely spot, and an unsuspecting duck was raised. The dog, who answered to the name of Happy, because he always seemed about to smile, was all set and at heel.

There was a hell of a din, as both barrels were loosed off. We looked around to see the dog in action as the duck descended from the skies, but he was nowhere to be seen. It was as if he'd just vanished, and no wonder. At that particular moment he wasn't earth bound. At the sound of the blast, he'd taken off in a skyward direction and was in the air for those split seconds, escaping our horizontal gaze. When he came back to earth, it was difficult for his paws to get traction, such was his terror and eagerness to be off. He skidded for the first few yards before gaining the desired rocket-like velocity. All this was accompanied by his agonised whelps. I was reminded of the characters in cartoons, where they seem to quickly fade over the horizon.

There was much repressed laughter, until I saw the look on his face. He was certainly not amused.

"Quiet".

Eventually we got everything back into the car, including the unlucky duck, and then father made his way to the hostelry from whence he'd acquired the dog. On peeping through the door, I could see him approach a man at the bar and, surprise, surprise, there was Happy sitting at his feet, supping up a bowl of food and he *did* seem to be quite *Happy*. I could just hear parts of the conversation, words like, "What sort of a dog is that?"

More words like, "When you sold him to me you said he was a great gun dog. I bang off a couple and he nearly shits himself and runs back to here. Does he like the beer or something?"

The man replied, "Ay, you mean old Homer. He is a bit of a homing bird."

"I don't care what you call him. You told me that he was Happy and a great retriever."

"Ah, he is." The face under the cap continued, "He retrieves me every time I sell him. I mean, it's not against the law to sell you the dog and then he decides to come back to me. He must prefer me to you. It's up to him, isn't it? I don't want him to stay now. You can take him with you again if you want. Take him out of here. Take him home. I mean, he's your dog rightly. After all you have bought him. He'll probably go with you, but it's not my fault if he wants to come back again. You could keep him chained up all the time, but he wouldn't like that and he'd cry a lot. You'd have the neighbours complaining." The voice droned on and on.

There was a further muttering and a very heated exchange. The upshot being that money was seen to change hands and so ended the retriever episode—Happy would live to be sold again another day.

Fall from Bike

There are such moments in a life, like the day when I fell off the bike. I had applied my brakes when I saw the old lady burdened down with shopping. She was struggling to cross near the top end of Grafton Street. It was as busy as ever, with motor cars and people rushing hither and thither, and there she was.

I thought to go to help her, as she seemed in some difficulty. However, on applying the brakes on my very old machine, I was thrown over the handlebars, because the front brakes had come on and seized as can happen in very old bikes. Not an altogether uncommon occurrence with bikes of such vintage. I went over the handlebars, hitting my head on the kerb, and they said it affected me thereafter. That's a matter of opinion.

But the old lady was very unsteady as she stumbled over me and the bike, her shopping and all on top of me. Now we are struggling together in some disarray to get to our feet and disentangle ourselves away from the wretched bike. We must have looked like something out of a comic strip.

Some of the younger ones standing in the bus queue thought that it was so funny. They were pissing themselves at my plight.

Dubliners have that rare sense of humour of laughing at another's misfortune. A very pretty girl, who had been waiting in the bus queue, had seen all and was not laughing. Our eyes met, though only momentarily, and that was a lifetime for me. That was it. I scrambled to my feet and, having regained my faculties, helped the old lady with her bags of shopping safely onto the kerb. The kindly girl, who had looked at me, was picking up my bike and held it for me. She asked, "Are you all right?"

"Yes, I think so, although I'm a little shaken and bruised. Thank you very much indeed for getting my bike."

All this was happening at the same time as I asked the old lady the same question while being thanked most profusely by her. She said, "I'm very grateful to you, young lad, and so sorry you fell when you were trying to help."

Then the young lady holding the bike said to me again, "Are you all right? Do be careful."

"Yes, I think I'll be all right, thank you."

"I'm glad you're not hurt."

"You're very kind."

She commented sympathetically, "I think everyone has a fall sometime. I fell off my bicycle a few weeks ago. I wish I'd had it with me today, instead of waiting for this bus which never seems to come."

Then as she turned to go back to the bus queue, she said, "I think I'll walk."

She didn't tell me her name, but in my mind I would call her Queenie."

I mumbled, "Would you mind very much if I walked along with you?"

I was surprised at myself as I continued, "It will give me a chance to collect myself. I don't feel like cycling for the time being."

In the meantime, the old lady was casting me more grateful glances as I walked away with my dream girl, who really did look regal and queenly with lovely long fair hair and dark brown eyes. I was captured, and no mistake. It just seemed as natural as falling off a log or a bike if you like, that I should be walking with this lovely creature. I said very little as we walked way past where I should have turned off. At last, it seemed, with some reluctance, she said, "I've got to take this turning, as I live down there, and thank you for walking with me."

She walked briskly away down towards the canal bank road. And that was it.

All I could say was, "Oh have you?"

What I really wanted to say was, "You're gorgeous. You're beautiful. I'd love to see you again, tonight, today, tomorrow, anytime you'd want to see me. I would worship at your feet, you lovely girl." And I thought how absurd it would all sound to blurt out anything so bloody stupid, breaking all the conventional taboos which strangled my vocal chords. So I just mumbled something incoherently like, "Goodbye, maybe I'll see you sometime."

As I continued alone, my mind was very pre-occupied indeed. I very nearly ran after her, but didn't.

To lie here and think about it, I blame myself for being thick to not at least have found out where she lived so I could see her again, but I knew, deep down in my subconscious, that she had taken pity on a sad-looking boy who had fallen from his bike while trying to help an old lady and could never possibly have any other interest in a being such as me. I've often thought about it.

Lying There

Why does my time just ebb away? Where's all that get up and go? Where's all that enthusiasm? It could be all a dream. I mean, life itself. Where does the real begin and the unreal end?

I should have gone to see her. There I go again. That could have been a dream. I might never have seen her at all. Are all the things you experience in a dream any less real in emotional terms at the time? Don't we feel them just the same, while it's all happening?

If I hadn't had my dreams, life wouldn't have been the same. Maybe what I thought was reality was the dream and vice versa. Now the question is whether to go out or not, stand still, lie down, do nothing, just think about her. I often thought about writing her the most poignant love letter with such pleading of my love for her that she couldn't fail to be moved. I would rush up to her and hand it to her before she could say anything, then I'd flee and wait for her to come running after me, pleading with me to stop, so that she might speak. And her voice would go faint in the distance, still hailing me as I ran and ran and ran. Why should she run after me?

All this speculation and I didn't even get her name, and there you go, so stop all this wishful thinking. Is it a deep-down fervent wish to assure me of something that she should overtake me while I was running and draw me back and crush me to her? It would be pure heaven on earth, pure ecstasy, truly a dream come true. I know that if she did that, I wouldn't know what to say. I would be just a gurgling mass of emotion within my misshapen shell, suffering the longing that couldn't bear expression. Oh, just to think of it makes me shiver and tremble all over. Does it all spring from a subconscious, like from when her back was turned. Is it all imprinted deep down? The more I think about it, the more ridiculous it seems. And yet, I do know she was with me and had my sole attention for that few moments when we walked.

So many times later when I cycled past the bus stop and then along the route where I thought she might be walking, I often thought that if I did see her, I would do my falling-off bit again, just to gain more sympathy.

As I fell, I'd exclaim in mid-air, "Here I go folks, just doing my old falling off trick for your entertainment. Don't hold back. Come on, you've all got to have a good f*****g laugh!"

It might have been better if I'd never met her, but then, what would I have thought about?

That part of my mind could possibly have been a blank. I'd never have been able to conjure up all the thoughts and all those unfulfilled conquests that can still hold a promise. I wished that I'd been better equipped to deal with the situation when I met her. I mean, falling off a bicycle. What a stupid way to meet someone. That piece of old junk, patched up and screwed together, had long since given of its better years. Who should have ever craved mobility on such a piece of mechanical scrap? And yet, only for that she would never have been there in my moment of distress.

The picture it must have presented was one of such obvious ill-founded lack of material possession on the one hand, and pure gaucheness on the other, and yet, she had walked those miles, I don't know how long. Perhaps I exaggerated; perhaps I stretched our walk into miles. It painted a picture for me of hope and I've got to cling to that because there must be some hope. There must be something, even if it's of my own invention. Perhaps she was just sorry for me, and when you're lying on the road, with a bike wrapped around your neck, anyone would feel sorry if they weren't laughing. Perhaps it was the old lady that she really felt sorry for. What does it matter? There I go again and why bother?

I'm wondering what to do about the whole thing and all I can deal in is subterfuge, mental and otherwise, and deviousness that won't work. Maybe it was never an accident at all, but the bicycle was the key factor in the whole episode. The detached mechanical pedalling machine to end my cycling days toppling over handlebars at the feet of an old lady and a kindly smiling queen, all the parts relating and yet so disconnected. The bike is synonymous with the queen, destined to bring that meeting together. All the nuts and bolts in its conception and manufacture had been aimed at me. The bike had been bought for me by someone who had the best possible intentions to get me out of myself, get me out of things, out of doors, out of sight, you might say. So you could say it was on doctor's orders after my first illness.

Ruminating

When you're lying in bed, standing up or sleeping, it doesn't matter and the many human souls who lie down with no muscle deployed can work it out quite easily. Like the bird that sleeps on one leg and is ready for the marathon flight the next day. We must be the most badly designed creatures who can lie down in comfort and rest not at all, feeling thoroughly exhausted on awakening.

When they learned of my bike mishap and saw the bruising, they must have had guilt feelings—they took it back to the cycle shop. There had been words about its defects and the money paid for it. The upshot being that it was completely overhauled and is like new, with spare parts fitted, and now I'm busy making all sorts of plans. Having had it restored, they were very keen to get me outdoors again. To get me out of myself. So here I am, back in the saddle, with face to the wind, straining against the elements. Those long adventure trips, always into the wind it seemed. To cycle, literally, for weeks (to escape from an imprisoned mental self) like a nomad on those long, hilly, winding narrow lanes that led to nowhere in particular, where one could be so alone with no questions to answer, with the feeling of being the only one on earth. One was sustained bodily on canned products, equipped with opener and spoon.

The bike for that period, was my open sesame to all the great open spaces beyond. So different to window prying. Peddling was a kind of relentless pursuit of an innocent voyage to find answers to what? When it rained heavily, my protection was the old, trusty, waxed commodious cape that still endured from its better military-use days, designed to keep a body dry in all outdoor weather. It had often been a friend to Cecil and me when we faced the elements together. After prolonged exposure, it would leak in its old seams, and softened candle wax would be rubbed onto the affected part, which did the trick. In extreme conditions, I sought cover under friendly trees. A fire of dry branches and a tin of beans could be warming. The reliable combustibles. What would the pedal-pushing pioneers ever do without the sustaining protein that produced the methane?

I'd lie secure in my sleeping bag close to the ever familiar earth, thinking to myself, *This is the life amidst the great outdoors.* I would then think to myself, *It's all bollocks!*

During my cycling period, I often peddled to the library, my world of make believe, to explore those far-flung dreams on the written page. Was that more bollocks? Living through other folk's dreams or scribing? Or was it the key to anywhere?

Am I the great watcher of all time? Like when I'd dawdle as I stared at the young girls coming from school. I ogled them with thoughts that the Holy Father would scarcely approve of.

In my peddling travels, I often visited the second-hand book shops. You could get old much-read classics, literally falling apart, for a few pence. They'd be so much read and used, with maybe a page or two missing, especially when you were coming up to some of the more interesting parts. You never knew from whose houses they came. That's the funny thing about old, well-read books: They all had a history of being sold, re-sold, and then back again to the second-hand shops, which had become a thriving industry in a city of a very poor but aspiring to be a literate and well-read people. They usually found their way into my possession when they were on their last legs and coming apart at the bindings and were for pennies. I loved reading about things of which I could only dream and imagine. The escapism while reading the page was a magical world of escape for so many.

More Window Prying

My ever-wandering and prying eye comprised a world of spying and looking, depending on the time of year. Late summer and autumn were best, at about 9:00 p.m. I would liken my eye to the shutter of a camera and, as I passed in the space of a few seconds or more, depending, while critically focusing my eye on the wide gap in unclosed curtains, like a focal plane, sear the picture on my mind and then analyse it as I peddled on. I expanded on the fleeting, condensed impression and conjure up my own image. I could even be involved in an imagined conversation with some fool who was in a privileged job, just for knowing someone in the political system, while indulging in an after-dinner brandy. It was a system that could at times be likened to the mafia. This was especially if any of your family had carried arms when the powers that be were in disagreement with John Bulls' governing system, now gone and part of a remembered tragic past. They were the favoured sons, those who shared the political pie with jobs in banks or civil service. Meanwhile, back at the windows, I'd feel, in my make believe world, that I'd been in their room and knew everybody inside. Then I'd leave the room behind and I'd be on the bike. Perspiration would gently steam from my forehead. It seemed that I was always peddling into a headwind toward an unfulfilled ending.

The once imperial windows of grand houses, all telling their different stories in those parts of a city in an island so full of culture and scholarship, and so much distress hidden away and wrong doing, often blurred by some in powerful positions which had become impregnable, against moral or fiscal discovery. It always happens when the gun is replaced by the lawful pen.

It's a long story of a once so-elegant Dublin, which had known better days. In many areas close to the centre of the city, those houses built and designed for large families with servants, now so multi-tenanted, told of a life of many who would never know other than large families sharing a tenement room in their faded magnificence.

It was an obsessive urge, it would seem, about calling on people. Why? I'd very slowly peddle past their houses and peer in as I passed, to see what I could see. I was a sort of a mobile Peeping Tom. I had no part of that life, which used to take place on the other side of mostly middle-class Georgian windows.

Now I'm just cycling past. The rain is misty. Maybe I'm moving too fast and don't get a good look. Some evenings when I seemed to have all the time in the world, I practically loitered on my machine and stared rudely into their private homes and lives without being invited. Sometimes, I'd draw a blank when nothing was happening inside. They couldn't be socialising all the time, just as I would be going past at those times in the evening, which were the most productive. The lights would be on and the curtains not fully drawn, so as to let the smoke from their pipes or cigars (depending on which part of the landscape your travels led) curl out on the evening breeze.

There were those preserved houses from a regency era, full of people talking to each other and sipping their wines and brandies as they dined.

From watching their mouths move in conversation, I could often grasp snippets of what they were saying. I evolved into a lip reader and their lips could tell me so much. I watched fascinated, sometimes with the use of old field glasses once owned by Big J's father when he wore a uniform during a dangerous period of our history, as many had. Big J used to carry them in his school bag, and they had somehow become mine all those years ago when we would view the landscape and other things we shouldn't from the lofty height of Cecil's rump.

Snippets of conversation could be like a puzzle when you tried to imagine what the whole story could be. When a women's moving lips was telling a scandalous story about another of their kind, it could be fascinating to learn that others sinned as well as I.

Once while sitting on my bike on one of my nocturnal patrols, I was window watching outside a house in Merrion Square. The curtains were open, and I was rudely staring at this sharp-featured, ample woman dressed in a revealing evening gown with glass in hand.

She seemed to be ranting at this man. From what I could read from her lips, she was talking about some girl from her office and saying that she was a right whore and had been out with the manager and they had stayed in the Hibernian Hotel for two nights. She then happened to look through the window and saw me sitting on the bike with the glasses and let out a holler and was shouting as I peddled furiously away. Looking into other people's windows was not without its hazards.

On party nights, there would be the extra help to cope with serving drinks and washing up and other such chores. The folk below stairs would get a running commentary from those serving above when they had to come below to fetch something or other and there would be comments such as, "Mr T is in good voice. He has had several stiff gins and is already getting f*****g slightly smashed." There was never a shortage of expletives among those below. I had a grudge against being deprived admittance to a society that would never accept me into its midst. Why? Would it have made me any happier?

No, it wouldn't. I don't know why, but I wanted to be on the inside. It was like looking at a part of life which would never involve me.

Back on the bike in the wintry landscape: When they were skating on the lake, I tried to ride amongst the skaters. I wanted to belong, but I skidded all over the place and wound up sitting on the ice. I then found great difficulty in getting to my feet. My voice nearly changed an octave as I doubled up in pain from the collision of the hard saddle into my groin area as I landed heavily.

A female kind soul asked, "Did you fall, young man?"

In agonised voice, "No, I always purposely get off the bike this way and have my bollocks paralysed."

She gave me as good as she got, when she retorted, "Ah, yes, so they must be. You always get off like that, do you, with the saddle stuck up your arse?"

It was a bit like when I used to get home after having been out on the bike most of the night, maybe window looking, or what she would call window snooping. She'd be waiting up, no matter what the hour and ask, "What time do you think this is?"

Then I think. It's time for her third degree routine. What a time for questions!

She knew I used to go window looking. She'd say, "You must stop this window looking. It's not healthy. It must be some kind of phobia."

She would continue: "You should keep away from people's windows. You're nothing better than a Peeping Tom. They talk about you and say you are so odd."

If it wasn't looking in, it was looking out. It was an obsession. I told her I was going to knock on their doors and say, "Good evening, Madam. What story is your window telling this evening? I can see that you have some people in your front room and I was wondering if you'd kindly tell me who they are.

Then the kindly, so-elegant lady would smile and say, "Well, it's so nice to have a young gent call on me and want my window story. Sure and bless you young man, I'll tell you all about it. Come on in, you've really made my evening. I was getting so bored with the company anyway. Would you like a glass of something? It really is very kind of you to pay a call upon us." She would continue, "You do look a real handsome fellow with your trousers tucked into your socks and the cycle clips and your cap pulled down over your ears. What a picture of the outdoors man you make. Do not worry about your bike. I'll get Jenkins to park it when he's finished with the guests. No doubt you would like me to tell you about my guests. I think we had better talk in private. What do you say we slip upstairs and I'll tell you first of all about myself? Don't you think that would be a lot more interesting?"

"Oh, yes, of course, and thank you, missus. You really are very kind. Yes, I'd love to go upstairs and listen to your story. I think everybody wants to tell their story don't you? You see, I want to hear everyone's window story. I'm a window-story man."

I'd be thinking all this to myself. Isn't it marvellous, everyone wants to take me upstairs and tell me their story with large glasses of lovely tasting liquid?

She asked, "What shall I call my window story?"

I suggested, "Life Cycles in Society?"

"Ah, yes. Life Cycles. Now isn't that something? And what shall I call you, dear boy?"

"Just call me Mal." And I'd be thinking like mad. Don't let me wake up to reality. Keep me transported.

Then she was saying, "Do you like the bedroom? I'll have Jenkins bring up some more Champagne when he's parked your machine. Get those cycling clips off and let some air up your legs. For God's sake, must you wear your cap indoors? Why don't you hang it on the bedpost knob? Now you've really got to listen to my story while I make you comfortable. Come on, loosen your tie. Unbutton your trousers. Do you think I have nice breasts? Yes, that's nice. You like holding them? Aren't they nice and firm and large? Oh, don't stop. Just keep sucking.

Haven't I got lovely nipples? You love the taste? Meeting you, young man, has been the answer to my prayers."

"Wake up. You're asleep again. Just look at the mess his bed's in. You take that side, while I fluff out his pillows. He's looking so peaceful. Where would we be without the ministering angels?"

People in Groups

People gather in groups to give themselves a sense of being secure, being part of or wanted or needed for survival, or even loved or whatever. I've mostly been a group of one. Talk to yourself and you're a group of one. Albeit, an odd one. As a child, to talk to yourself is quaint and amusing to adults, but if you continue to do as you get older, they'll frown with questioning looks. They'll say that there is something very odd about your mental processes.

I have to constantly discuss many things with myself. Who else is there to talk to most of the time?

Nature, the great group planner, never intended us to be solo. She believes in strength in survival by volume. The loss rate being catered for by numbers. She accepts that she will be forgiven for a lot of rejects, even like me, which come off the production line.

Snooping from the Trees

At a much later time in an introspectively confined life, I would be intrigued, as I was still watching or snooping from a vantage point among the bordering trees at that time of evening when business would be brisk for the revellers and others who would need their services, when the women rented their bodies to prospective clients.

For the most part, they showed the wear and tear in their visage of constant confrontation with the risk element in a promise to fulfil the appetites of frustrated souls.

Faces once so young and pretty would all have their particular story to tell. Their tale was nearly always the same in that they had someone or other who had let them down badly in their lives or had got them hooked on forbidden substances, left them with a baby and no one to care. They were obliged, in order to survive, to do it, to live and keep the issue and body alive in the oldest profession.

They said that some of them liked the adventure and risk and enjoyed doing it. There was a new one among the group. I hadn't seen her face before.

She had yet to chalk up the mileage which would inexorably change her into the vixen who would try to survive the daily body traffic, never to be spared in satisfying the biological demands of many.

There was such fascination in my voyeurism, as I wheeled my bike in among the cover of the trees, observing all the while, from my vantage point among the bushes close to the traffic in that city with the huge green at the centre of all that would be happening as dusk descended on the parks and the hotels and attendant traffic near the centre of busy thoroughfares, a city with all its ills and pleasures to be catered for.

The huge green was named after St Stephen, who would frown on many of its nocturnal aspects, which afforded a much needed relief for some. Thoughts flooded back to when I watched through the curtains of the cottage in times long past.

The new as yet innocent face had a kind of beauty in her vulnerability as she looked around nervously, like a new-born foal, whose instincts told her that she would have to be ever watchful and fearful at not knowing what might be in store.

The older ones were showing her how to make the best approach to prospective clients. Walk alongside the slow moving, park-side traffic and pick out the likely punters for a possible trade.

I could see them showing her how to waggle her hips in a short tight skirt, in an exaggerated fashion, even to the detail of swinging her hand-bag casually. There was no need to hear what they were saying, because the mimicry was perfect.

I usually chose a time for my voyeuristic activities when trade was at its busiest, which would usually be around about 11:00 p.m., *après* dinner and pub drinking times from the nearby hotels and well-known watering holes with foreign military visitors on leave escaping from the war.

I could indulge myself in those fantasies for the most part, for in my mostly impecunious state, I could only watch. I wanted to speak to the new girl. The others were now away with punters—one might even call them clients—who would get relieved during a short, most-intimate but brief liaison.

It was curious to observe and be fascinated by the many approaches from would-be clients, as she walked away each time. She seemed so timid and lost. Another man came by and said something and she walked away again. The man shouted some obscenity after her. She now walked very rapidly and was heading towards my vantage point. I could see her face clearly. She was a kitten with eyes full of tears.

She wasn't more than about fourteen years of age, a mere child. Her clothes were so short, the tight skirt revealed the as yet untrammelled limbs.

As she drew level with my position, I came from the cover of the trees and startled her. She gave a gasp. "What do you want? What d'ya mean coming out like that? Gave me a fright, you did. What are you, some kind of freak or something? Were you spying on me?"

I stuttered and stammered, "No, I 'er. I mean. I wasn't doing anything."

Big Sadie was now returning to her pitch and as she approached, I quaked. She was the queen Madame of the "Girls" on her patch. She controlled them for the boss man. As she came up to us she laughed and said, "You'll not get a tip from this one. He's as weird as they come. He's always watching and spying on us. Bring him over here and let's see what he's made of. Somehow I let myself be brought to where the girls had reassembled after their various assignations. They brought me farther in among the trees as they gathered around, as if to inspect this curiosity. Big Sadie grabbed me and said, "You weren't going to tell on our little sister were you? I think you should be her first customer."

They all laughed as they crowded in closer. The new girl was looking on with a bemused expression and she kind of whimpered, "It wasn't my fault. I just saw him coming out from among the bushes."

Then Sadie's imperious voice: "Bring him over here." She winked at the other girls as they gathered to enjoy their little playful distraction.

They were now bent on having some fun to liven up the direness of their trade as I shivered in anticipation tinged with fear. They had now brought me deeper in among the night dark foliage, well away from the road. They were passing a bottle among themselves and swigging its strong contents.

Big Sadie was saying, "Come on, girls, let's see what the lad's got."

A million hands seemed to be grabbing my trousers and taking them off. It made me think of those swarms of ants with but one object in view. As they forced me into a reclining position, their faces crowded in over mine and they were so close I could smell the stale perfume from their bodies of toil. Many hands were exploring my sensitive areas. Sadie bent over me, her big breasts heaving across my face, and she looked at me and drew her very heavily made up face so close to mine, and her great rouged lips sucked and kissed. I convulsed in that ecstatic agonising trauma as I gushed. She exclaimed, "Ah, I think we've brought forth the first water, have we not? Don't worry, there's plenty more where that came from, isn't there, girls?"

So many of them now, all laughing and giggling, stroking me with the skill of long experience, sending me into areas of sensation which drew on so many memories. Then a rather diminutive older one called Gladys remarked, "You always did like a bit of bent, didn't you, Sadie dear?"

Another one gazing at my parts commented, with the air of one who had assessed many, "I've not seen such a pretty little one for years."

Could all this be really happening? Although frightened, I was amazed at me for being so submissive to their desires and me frighteningly enjoying it. Then Sadie: "Go on, give him a kiss, Gladys. Who's going to be first?" And elderly Gladys bent down to kiss me so full and wet as she sucked hard to evacuate my engorged electrode. I remember gazing into a face that had been once so pretty. My long lost queen had kissed me like that many years ago on the fateful day, when she had discharged me from her life. It rekindled it all again. Then raising herself up from her labours, she put her tongue deep into my mouth and I nearly gagged. Was I helpless or fascinated? Her long jet black hair fell over my face and then over my thighs as her area of interest was re-directed once more. *Oh not again, oh God.* As my system convulsed, she drew back laughing with all the wet on her face. Now they were laughing uproariously and enjoying the basic function of their toy as she spat it on my face. Then it was Sadie's turn once more. She was stroking me all over. Could this really be? Was I alive? Then she said to the new girl, "Come on, young Esther, it's your turn," and there they were again. Esther was saying, "Oh, no, not me, please."

Sadie commanded, "It's got to be you. He's going to be your first customer. You've got to start somewhere, and at least this will be a safe experience."

They lifted her off her feet. They were enjoying some light relief in their otherwise sordid life as they let their whims take hold. They laughed aloud when they saw that she had pants on. "You don't wear those in our business my child," Sadie was telling her. "Get them off."

It seemed like many talons quickly removed her modest undergarment. She was raised above me and then lowered very slowly, it seemed, onto the inevitable. It was as if she levitated, as her descent was carefully controlled. She seemed to float down onto me. Sadie was stage managing the whole event. "Oh, no, oh no," Esther moaned in her agony, as they kept pressing her down and down, her moans subsiding as she sank lower and lower, and I was piercing and piercing until it seemed that we were bonded in an oscillatory union. Ever fainter and fainter her sighs became and then almost inaudible. Then everything seemed to dissolve into a beautiful haze and all matter was freed from suspension.

Her face against mine was deathly pale as she lay astride with the entire world spent. We lay comatose, with her first blood upon me. It was eerie as they were now all so still and silent.

After what seemed an age, they lifted her from me. Sadie pulled me to my feet saying, "You won't need to spy again, will you?" She then started to shake me and shake me. "Now, you know what it's like, we'll not be having any hole in the corner spying. You come along and take your medicine like the rest of them, okay?" She kept shaking me and shaking, and I could hear my mother's voice as my eyes opened. It wasn't Sadie's big bust bending over me, just a mother yelling, "Come on, come on. It's time you were up. Are you going to lie there all day, just daydreaming?"

Mind Puzzles

Later on, the man trained to understand the function of our minds would sit by his couch and listen, as he explained to me the ramifications of the Freudian dream. It dated back to the time when I'd followed Monica and Jill. I'd resented his easy mental probing that seemed to make me tell all, and I was resentful at having told him so much about myself and my most personal thoughts.

Come on, why don't you just switch yourself off for once. We should be our own determiners and should be able to end it all, pull the plug and problems no more. What freedom to be detached and float in a restful void. But maybe that's only an extension of the dream and the dream's a reality.

The younger dreams were so much more interesting. But always at the most exciting part, somebody would pull the plug to rudely awake me back onto this mortal coil. "Get up, boy, you're late, you're always late." How often have I heard that?

And it's far too late now, with things to do. All thoughts of what might have been to be put away, sublimated, dismissed for more mundane acts of function.

A mother awakening her son will never know how many joyful dreams she has thwarted or those she has prevented from enjoying a fruitful conclusion, when about to be in receipt of a fulfilling experience.

In those early years, life seemed too full of such awakenings. All such young saplings, who sublimely sported members so perky and erect, would always remember those frustrating rude awakenings.

Big J at school never seemed to have any difficulties in that area. He just followed his desires in bodily learning, exploratory fumble, and discovery by instinct.

I wondered if animals had those sorts of dreams. Nobody teaches you to dream in the first place. No-one ever shows you how to do it. You just lie down, sleep takes over, and you're there. It's a miracle. It's the other world of the unconscious-subconscious, which can allow free play. That thrilling book of dreams where there was always catastrophe about to strike, where one was about to be preyed upon, or be thrown from or dashed to pieces, or a head to be chopped, or a hangman's noose about to be stretched taut, or perhaps you're about to pierce the queen, "Wake up lad, wake up." And yet once again you were saved, or deprived of your prize, in the prick of time.

Come back to the question. Should I end it and enter into a new landscape? Maybe I could be in new surroundings with different parts to play. Does pulling the plug determine the end of the dream or the beginning of a new dream world of a promised hereafter, or will it just go blank? To steer the ship of one's own finality, thus finalising the account in the supposedly real world. But I expect that there's got to be those further promised lands ahead, like The Holy Father of his flock had promised so often in his teaching and shaping of the very young minds in his care.

The Leaves

Hold on a minute, I'll adjust this pillow. Ah, that's more comfortable. When I told them I wanted to throw snowballs in the bedroom, it had been snowing for days, and days, and they didn't think it was funny. People are throwing them outside. It was all right, to look through the window and watch the others. It all seemed great fun. But no, they wouldn't bring in some snow, just for me to have a throw. I'm getting tired of being in here. I want to be back among my old friends, the leaves. I wonder if they'd give me my old job back and let me try once more, be given another chance of usefully being occupied by a caring City Corporation. A municipality looking after us all and its own secure jobs and pensions.

It seems as if I've always been going to see someone or other. I often wondered if I'd ever arrived or ever got to where I was going. Although I'd kidded myself I'd arrived many times. When I did, I probably never realised it. The most over-riding mental picture is of non-arrival, though arriving unexpectedly can lead to other things.

When they let me out, it seemed that they had worked their magic on me and I was once again fit to be among them and at my most perceptive. I was deemed to be no longer a threat to shipping. They said I could now mingle in society and even call at houses and try to sell them the books that knew all the answers.

During my quite brief book-selling period, I always expected that when a small man came to answer the door bell, I would instinctively look for the big lady. Why?

He would have just come from his place of work. The Britannica are on the shelf. He's late thirties, probably well read, like many of his time, with a big mortgage and not a lot of money to spare.

He is looking hard at me and my battered old brief-case, which has chalked up so many miles by so many previous aspiring failures before me. It had been given to me by a despairing mother who would give her problem child some hope of doing something useful in a hard commercial world of books sold on commission, wearing a suit previously owned and cleaned.

The householder was irked by my intrusion and anxious to get on with reading his paper. Although an appointment of sorts had been made from the office, it didn't lessen his mood, and he is asking why should I be taking up his valuable time?

He said in a tired and contained tolerant voice, "If you would just run through it briefly."

He continued in the same vein, a kind of command for *Let's have your story, go through it, get on with it quickly before big momma puts my evening meal on the table.* "Yes, by all means, sit down. Don't mind if I potter about a bit while you're speaking? Yes, I'd better switch the wireless off. You won't want that going on while you're talking. Well, I'll turn it down and have it in the background."

You think to yourself, *Yes, sure why not? Maybe I should just * * * * off and save my breath.* It made me feel like an interloper.

And so it went in other people's houses. Suffer the frustration of repeated failure. Young and eager, or just young and stupid, and why bother putting his signature on an order form out of sheer desperation when you know it'll be cancelled.

You can imagine the scenario much later, when the parcel arrives.

"Who sent these bloody books? I never wanted them."

Then there is the depressing feeling of wasted time and effort, when the commission is deducted from your pittance.

Another promising career of approximately some weeks ending in complete frustration, once again at having failed where others had made it to management. Why didn't they look upon it as a feat of great magnitude? Have a presentation dinner and say, "We'd like you to receive this gold watch as a token of your great efforts and non-achievement. And at the same time, May we please have the two pounds commission back, which we paid you in advance. Oh, yes, and if you are not going to need that old briefcase now, we could use it for the next mug."

Wouldn't a watch have been something to show for a very short selling career? Who made them think, even for a very brief moment, that I might be part of the world of commerce? All this, after they'd given me their treatment and pronounced me fit to cope, when I had eventually put their puzzle together.

You have failed yet another test. Why has there always got to be a test. Even the queens make you go through their test.

There's no satisfaction without fulfilment. Why do you need satisfaction? It is because you exist? Exist for what? You don't know. Nobody ever told you for what purpose, other than the procreative (only allowed under their conditions), but there's got to be more than that, and you're always hoping.

When you're ten, you hope that at fifteen things may be better, and at fifteen you're hoping that by the time you're twenty all things will have sorted themselves out. Then, when they are not so good at twenty, you think, *maybe twenty-five. Okay, wait 'til thirty?* Then you get to forty and probably you're happier after forty because you're not expecting so much. There is not the blind optimism of the very young and untried.

Most of it has gone. But the human animal is not built that way, and you start to assess values in their true sense, possibly for the first time. It doesn't mean that all your optimism goes, but you temper it with speculative and nervous reservations that, you know from previous disappointments, are necessary.

Of course, you're mindful of the fact that you've turned the middle of the road and you've turned down from the camber, and time is not of the plentiful supply it once was. Yes, that's it: you rationalise and come to grips with certain things or values. Then the years seem to come and go that much faster, and they come and go, and they go from where we are begun, and go right back to the umbilical who severed me from the womb where I'd slept enshrouded, back to the question: why disgorge an imperfect issue?

From that moment everything deteriorates. You may get bigger, as the seeds are getting larger, and atomising the bits that make your frame, from the first slaps on your bottom that made you give your first cry to the world to let them know you're here. All part of the regurgitating process when joy was the cup they poured. They poured all they'd got. Aunts and uncles visiting came to look at a beautiful baby. So curious to see, but not to hear?

Don't these people realise I need my sleep? Stop lifting me up every five minutes. Let them all smile or weep for a birth.

Let them cosset me, this brief spell before my first cast-off and spurning. That's where it started; it shouldn't have happened. I should have stayed in the womb, miss-shaped and malformed. Why issue, why discharge misshapen tissue?

Can I really remember the forceps? Yes, the forceps, as they fastened on to grip with supposedly professional hands. No consultation with me about how to use that instrument. Sometimes it was not used with the necessary expertise and left its lasting legacy and birthmark, to be there forever, in a disfiguring process from their tools of deliverance. The point of leaving and arriving and the discharging, outstretching, ever detaching, over appending, and the supply line now detached forever. What was it all for? Why be born if not perfect? Why no second chance? My early queen should be brought before their court to explain it all. She could tell them of my initial education, presided over by her, and of her rules, and our Pastor who taught me to play His sacred game of life, which must always be played within his strict rules, or you would be banished forever.

She could explain the pain that we're all supposed to suffer in order to play the game. And when he kept telling me that I would be banished if I didn't conform, then how could I enjoy that game as played by my queenly mentor of former times?

When she mocked me in disdain, I'm sure she didn't mean it to end like it did.

A most humiliating experience was to bring forth subsequent irrational actions. She would never know what damage she did to me. It's simply that there is always something in the memory compounding another something that forms the pattern.

So, cast your imperfect ones aside, as society and convention imposes its rules, so that it can function, in that it accepts that it is not perfect. It's what society does, and it does it cleverly as time progresses, depending on the degree of imperfection. Otherwise, what was to be done with those imperfects which come off the assembly line from time to time? There must be places to hide them away.

Should human fruit be allowed to suffer and meander into slow decay, subjected to the vicarious pleasure of an imperfect society? They don't say it in so many words, but it's there, and you're looked upon with complete reservation because you don't quite fit. You are to be viewed with a degree of tolerance and curiosity.

Then there are the pleasures to be enjoyed by one or other of their number when they adopt you for one of their whimsical sideshows and dropped again when their period of twisted perversions have been sated and their transient pleasure has passed. Discarded like the pet they feel no longer inclined to keep. So go back into your dream-world, it's the only world that's inviolate and where you're allowed freely to travel and commit such heinous crimes against them as you wish, without any redress or consequences. Then to awake to conforming strictures which might inhibit one pursuing those outrageous adventures which transported you in another life.

Clearing the Leaves

It was after another long day, well into the evening as dusk set in after I'd been clearing those leaves. I sipped from my bottle among the trees at the Green. Some habits never change. I watched the hurrying traffic and people all going about their business. As the same old distilled fluid circulated in my bloodstream, I felt a bit better as dusk was settling in, observing the nightlife of a people with the usual appetites in that twilight world of a society which felt more guilty than it should, but always pretended that it wasn't there. I would be sitting there with my bottle, watching the goings on, as they say. Here I was again, doing what the Holy Father had very firmly told me, "Was very bad for me and staining my blessed soul."

So many miles have been crossed in life since those days when I would kneel in trepidation in his darkened box and confess all. I think back and become cynical, knowing now when I watched that I just found it interesting in a quirky clinical sort of way, knowing that by merely watching, I was breaking his rules. But I couldn't help it.

I just liked watching the lives of others and what they did.

While observing those female much-trammelled camels of The Green, I still found it fascinating as they dispensed their services to those who could pay. There were those who could afford extra for their particular kind of fulfilment. During my time spent observing from the cover of the bushes and trees, I had come to know a woman by the name of Steph the Hip. Because she was so tall and once shapely, her slight limp as she walked was more noticeable. We had become sort of friends, as it would seem that we were both just a little odd. She seemed to like oddities and people that certainly were not the norm, and so it was that she had entered my life. For some obscure reason, she liked talking to me as I sat among the trees. In time, we got to know each a bit better and would even on occasion have a sip from my bottle when it would contain a good drop, as she would on occasion comment after a sup. It was at such times when her services were not required elsewhere, comforting some lonely soul in need of her special therapeutic gifts.

So when there were no punters about, she didn't seem to mind my little harmless proclivities for watching others go through their lives. She could be very quirky, and the women who worked the area all knew she was a one off, and so it was that sometimes Steph would talk to me when I was ensconced in my corporation-issue duffle with hood under a friendly evergreen while sipping the amber sauce after I'd spent another long day with the leaves and other no hopers.

She would say things like, "How is it cutting, Mal?" Then, if she was in the mood, she would have a good sip and after several more, "How would you like me to give you a nice squeeze down in the bargain basement."

And then, looking at my shy nervous enquiring face expressing my pleasurable anticipation, as in a child about to receive a new toy, I would say, "Oh, yes, Stephy, please. I would love you to do it, But you know, I never have—"

And before I would finish my sentence, she would cut in. "You should know me by now, my little freakish friend. You don't have to worry. For you, it's on the house," and she would start her magic in among those old friendly trees. She would deploy her tongue and when I was being transported, she would squat upon me and rub her oozing wetness over me, and before long, I would be discharging my pent up full udders into her writhing body.

How she could work her magic with such expertise with those same hands and lips that had relieved so many grateful souls. When I was similarly relieved she'd say, while wiping herself between her legs with a huge tissue (she always seemed to have a supply), "Wasn't that lovely? Let's go down to Ryan's and have a good drop."

I never refused her invitation and was always surprised at the apparent interest she seemed to take in what I did. She always was well in funds and would buy me a drink and ask about the work and the leaves in the parks. She was quite statuesque and spoke in a posh accent. As a child she had grown up in London and was one of those hopeful ballet dancers at Saddlers Wells.

I couldn't help but get the impression that she had been sinking a few with a client before she had seen me. As if reading my thoughts, she said, "I've spent most of the day with a most generous political gentleman in a lovely suite in Jury's Hotel. He is a regular, and he told me that he loved the things I could do that made him feel alive again."

I made no comment and as we sat at the corner table and drank the black stuff chased by Jameson, she looked at me and smiled in an indulgent way. She said, "Mal, you never ask me how I got my bad hip?"

Without waiting for my answer, she continued, "It's what most of them do. They enquire and say, 'Did you have an accident?'" She went on, "I always say yes, that I fell off a horse when young at the riding school. I took the full weight as his hoof caught my hip. It fractured and never mended properly. But, as you may have guessed, it is not what really happened, but I'll tell you the true story."

Her speech had become slightly slurred at this stage and I was very keen indeed to know what happened as I nodded in anticipation, "Go on, tell me what happened."

"I'll tell you, Mal, because I know you'll not tell another soul."

I looked at her and smiled and thought again about how she had swayed a bit unsteadily earlier when she had walked over to me at the Green among the trees. It was obvious, even to me, that she was now well topped up from the said client she had mentioned earlier. It would seem he had been quite generous when paying for her excellent services. As I thought this, I knew that her tongue might never be so loose again.

Her posh voice was just a bit more slurred as she said, "You see, it was so many years ago, would you believe that I was doing some ballet dancing?"

I had vaguely heard her story somewhere about how she could dispense a very special service, although she was now past an age when her once beautiful face and athletic figure had become timeworn and much faded from her activities in the course of dispensing those moments of pleasure to those in need of her services while always enjoying a good drop from the bottle. It's all wear and tear I was thinking.

She continued, "You know, Mal, my proper name is Stephanie and although I was born in Dublin, my parents took me to England when I was a mere babe, long before the war. I had showed great promise as a dancer when very young, and they had got me into a small school of dance in the East End of London where my progress was very good for such a young girl."

She continued, as I just kept nodding attentively.

"It was when the war started and the blitz was in full swing. My parents were killed when one of the Luftwaffe's huge bombs blew up most of the street where they lived in Whitechapel. I escaped death, because I was away at ballet school. I was heartbroken, but my ballet teacher told me that I must keep going and work hard at my dancing, which I did.

"I then went to live with my aunt from Galway, who lived in Kings Cross. She had worked in London since the Great War, into the twenties, when the troubles were going on here. Later, as my dancing progressed, I had so impressed them that I was given an audition and then a job with The Saddlers Wells Ballet Company."

I was intrigued. "So what happened then?"

"It was not too long after that when I had my accident, and I'll tell you the truth, Mal, how it happened. You know I like all things quirky."

As she said this, she smiled at me. She was steadily sipping, and her posh voice was becoming even more slurred as more drink was brought to the table. She dipped into her large commodious, top-quality leather bag with a famous maker's name and pulled out a wad of notes. Pulling one off the roll, she gave it to Big Sean the barman and told him to have one himself and to keep the change. He smiled gratefully.

"Thank you very much, Miss Steph." He went back to serving others.

She nodded after Sean and commented, "I like Sean, and I even like you, you little oddity." I couldn't help thinking that Sean may have enjoyed some therapy from the fair Steph in the way they seemed to be at ease with each other.

And so she went on. "It happened because when I would meet someone big and interesting, I would seek an extra thrill, because I liked big men in every sense of the word. On one particular evening, having performed in the chorus of *Swan Lake*, I had taken a taxi from Saddlers Wells to the Café Royal in Regent Street. While enjoying a glass there, I had espied a big American soldier, whose ancestors had come in times long past from the African continent. He was now a captain in the American Army on leave in London.

"He was seated at a table near me and our eyes met. I flashed a kindly smile at this Othello, and it wasn't long before Captain Derek joined me at my table, and, you don't need to guess, that it wasn't too long before we had supped and dined and were on our way to his hotel. He never stopped looking at me, and I knew he was rearing to go.

"At that time I was so supple in all departments as a requirement of doing my ballet routines that I used to get a big thrill of anticipation when I would meet a suitable subject to give them my speciality, like my hip treatment. I could bend in so many ways, like you wouldn't believe. It was no strain for me to put my leg straight up vertically over the shoulder of a potential lover when standing face to face and bring him so close."

I was fascinated as she went on.

"I used to make them aware of my possibilities by doing things with my body, so they never forgot."

She paused and raised her glass of Jameson chaser and said, "Good luck." I raised mine in response and said, "Go on, tell us what happened."

"As it turned out," she continued, "it would seem that nature had endowed this brave soldier way above the normal issue in the downstairs department and it came to pass that when we were in his hotel room as more drinks flowed, that he was busting to go. I could see that he was now very aroused and anticipating those magical moments my supple body had in store for him. We cuddled and soon were getting hastily undressed, each admiring the other's form and especially Derek's lower massive dog tags as he moved in now fully ready for the act."

I whispered excitedly, "Yes, yes, go on."

She smiled and continued, "There I stood with my back to the huge wardrobe invitingly. I raised my leg even higher to facilitate his entry into me. He went in so deep with my leg straight up over his left shoulder and he thrilled me with his strenuous movements deep inside. I could feel and knew he was enraptured as he experienced such joyous relief.

"For that magical moment, we were locked in time. The earth did move. Then, while at his peak, for my quirky act, I lifted my leg even higher still as he went even deeper, and then, for my final *pièce de résistance*, I snapped down my raised limb on his so engorged member and heard a dull cracking noise as my hip painfully dislocated."

I was spellbound. "And then what?"

"Then, what indeed, you may ask. Whatever way it had dislocated, it has never naturally reset, which is what has left me with a small permanent limp so that even today, after all those years and many more miles on my clock, the girls still refer to me as Steph the Leg."

I could just look at this most unusual, once-beautiful woman and think that each one of us has some cross to bear.

After a brief silence, she got up from the table and said, "I've got to be off. I have a good punter lined up, but you have another."

She went to the bar, Spoke with Sean, adjusted her dress, and, amazingly, seemed to shrug the drink off and walked smartly out into the night.

Sean was smiling far too knowingly as he put drinks onto the table. He said half to himself while looking at me, "Steph is truly a one off."

Later Times and Skirmishes

I was coming to that age called the late middle of the road and seriously on the lookout for someone who could possibly be a true friend to someone like me, which is how I met up with those two when I had popped into Ryan's for my usual livener after another long day with the leaves.

I sometimes used Gaffney's. Public houses were like sociable watering holes where I would spend those times sipping the black stuff, always depending on my meagre resources. It was always with the thought, subconsciously, that you might meet others of like bent, or others who might even be similarly afflicted? Most of them were not very interested in meeting me. Who would want a sweeper of leaves?

They said I was more or less cured. But then was I ever cured? Among a certain element of my fellows, I seemed all right. The print-out which they did on my mind at that place said so, although my body denied it. I was still and always would be a suitable case for their treatment, but would be allowed to move harmlessly in certain areas of society. Was I free again? I think so, because they let me go back to my old job with the park keepers, for the powers that be kept places of employ for people like me. They rightly thought that it was a better choice than to have to keep us doing nothing useful in confined institutions, just as long as we posed no threat to society.

So at the end of another day of sweeping up millions of autumn leaves and feeling quite tired, I found my way to the Duke Street hostelry of refreshment to enjoy the waters of Saint James's Wells as produced by Sir Arthur's massive brewing establishment. To think that one could be knighted and join the nobility on the basis that you could make, for the most part, a deprived people happy through drink whilst making enormous profits.

I sat there quietly at the corner table, ruminating on matters, when a flower seller came in and sat at the other side of the table adjacent to me, under which she shoved her basket, wherein a few faded blooms remained.

I could see from her tense unhappy brow that she had also had another hard day of selling her wares at the top of Grafton Street near the entrance to The Green with not so many trees as in yesteryear. Again I remembered from long since, all those years ago, when war was raging in Europe and I, as a mostly innocent soul, would observe men with military uniforms being made happy for a brief time before going back to risk their lives in foreign lands.

She smiled kindly across at me and very soon I knew I would speak to her and she would take a glass of the malted black with me. She wouldn't be older than her late thirties. She had a face that had once been very pretty, but had seen its share of suffering at the hands of a society that often did not care when you had been abused, because it was a society that hid most of its dirty linen away from those who were better off for not knowing about it. It was a society very reminiscent of times past, when they had the power of "Inquisition." It was a society, ruled for the most part by our Pastors who wore "His cloth" and who knew best what was good for us in the saving of our souls.

There was still a spark in her lovely blue but tired eyes. Under her well-worn shawl she wore a low cut blouse, which was full of breasts, which she didn't mind me gawking at. I was always, such a gawker.

When a few pints of the black stuff had passed her lips, she told me how she had been orphaned when both parents had died from Tuberculosis. Her aunt had let her live in a leaky outhouse until she ran away to Dublin, where she had got a job working night and day in a large house near Merrion Square. She told me she had been forced to please the man of the house. He would give her money every time he did it and she had kept quiet.

But later, when he had caused her to be with child and the lady of the house found out, she had been cast adrift and had to go to The Saint Vincent de Paul, a most helpful charity that had saved many impoverished families. They washed and clothed her, then sent her to the nuns, who would help with the forthcoming baby.

The nuns had made her work so hard that when the time came her frail body couldn't cope. They took the dead child away and treated her as if she had committed a crime. There was no sympathy for her. Several months later when she had recovered some of her health, she thought she must get out of this place or she would die.

And so it was, that in the middle of one night, she put on her clothes, such as they were, and, in desperation, dropped out of the small-room window at the back of the institution, where she landed on the soft earth of the vegetable patch. No bones were broken, and she had staggered to her feet and made her way to the city.

She practically lived on the streets and begged outside the big hotels, having to sometimes do things for men that were repulsive so she could survive in a landscape of destitution, hunger, poverty and no other means of support. For that period of her life, she had been fully exposed to every vice of a rampant city full of people in similar plight, and somehow she was managing to get by. Then one night, as she was huddled in a doorway, a kindly man, who had put a pound note into her bowl, asked if she had nowhere to sleep. She nervously told him that she slept in doorways and places where those with nowhere to go took their night's rest, even on a park bench if there was nowhere else. She told me that there would be drunks and other beggars and attempted intimacies, which she sometimes had real trouble fending off. She told me that this man, one Joe Snode, gave her the address of a house just off Patrick Street and told her to go there and speak with Mrs Maher and tell her Joe had sent her.

Mrs Maher was indeed a most good and Christian lady. She was well known for helping those in distress. Her big old house, which had seen better days, was full of people who depended on her for a night's shelter.

I was agog and asked what happened next. She looked at me very hard, and her gaze strayed over to the bar and she said, "I'd gladly buy you one back, but I've only got enough for a half, which I was going to have on my own."

Then looking at my surprised face, she said a little anxiously, "That is, if it's all right with you. I've had a bad day. Nobody was buying any flowers. Not even my few regulars."

My first thought was that this woman could put the black stuff away, and that a portion of my meagre saved wages had already slipped down her throat by now. But like the lemmings, my curiosity was such that I nodded to Dave and we were soon having another.

Then she told me that Mrs Maher let her come and sell her flowers, as she more or less pleased. She was very understanding.

"She really liked me," she continued. "There was always a big pot of porridge made every morning. My health was a lot better than when I was with the nuns, although I had to sleep on a mattress in the cellar. It was the only space she had left. The house seemed to be packed with the dross of society, who all seemed to need help, but at least I felt reasonably safe.

Mrs Maher, she said, continuing her tale, while taking a large gulp from the refilled glass, told her that Joe was always helping people in trouble, and that he was like a saint.

Then she told me that, when the household was asleep, she would sneak out late at night through the little cellar door, which led onto the back garden, and take flowers from the gardens of the big Georgian houses near the square and sit at the gate to the Green and sell them next day. She found that she had to wander farther afield as her little business grew, until it happened in the early hours that a Garda asked her where she was going with the flowers and she had no proper answer. Then she was asked how she had come by them, and she couldn't explain properly.

Being a kindly family man with children of his own, he could only point out the grave error of what she was doing and that, normally, she would have to answer before the law.

However, he did very severely warn her off. It seems that this kindly guardian of our peace told her that she could still sell her flowers, but she would have to buy them. That was how, through another flower seller in Moore Street, she was able to sell her flowers mostly within the law, after having been guided through certain formalities allowed by the most helpful Corporation of Dublin to do so under licence.

I could see that her glass was nearly empty and her looking at me in such a way that I had no option but to wave at Dave across the mahogany and give a nod. Her face glowed as new filled glasses were once again on the table.

She smiled a grateful smile.

"You're very kind."

"Go on. Tell me more," I urged.

"Selling the flowers is hard. Some days there's not very much profit, in return for long and late hours, sometimes in the very cold winter months, I nearly freeze."

She said that saintly Joe Snode had saved her life in so many ways. He had encouraged her to go and try to make a living, such as it was, selling the flowers. Unlike other men, he never expected anything in return, but he once said that he valued the friendship of every hardworking girl.

The matronly, once good-looking Mrs Maher always seemed to smell of freshly washed linen, but sometimes there was a scent of whiskey on her breath. She would always repeat that Joe Snode was a saint on this earth and his place was assured in the next life.

Meanwhile, while I listened to her narrative, my mind had gone into a kind of overdrive, as I was thinking: *Could this quite attractive flower seller, who said her name was Marie, possibly identify with someone like me?*

She interrupted my thoughts. "How about you? What do you do?"

I thought it must be plain for her to see and observe me in my old worn duffle, that I was not a successful stock-broker? When I had told her most of it, leaving out certain parts, she had said a little glibly, "You could have possibilities, Mal. You speak nicely. But would you have the will-power?"

Did she mean it? I kept asking my unsure self. I dearly wanted someone. My thoughts were, from times past, that maybe I was better on my own. I was thinking of past disasters, no doubt. That was it. Was I happier on my own? Was I happier with my own weaknesses, without complications? Sometimes my weaknesses took over, and sometimes too much imbibing of the black stuff to forget the other stuff of life. It's all relative. And that's where she came into my story.

When he came into the bar, I saw the way she looked at him. They knew each other very well indeed. She said to me as she finished the drink, "Would you excuse me for a moment? My friend Barney has turned up and he wants to have a word."

She got up from the table and went over to the bar where he had ordered some drinks, and her glass was full again. They were in deep conversation. It was plain to see the situation. As things turned out, they would have a bit of fun with good old simple Mal. I told myself to walk well away, but I always made bad decisions where possible queens were concerned. As my mind was racing with all sorts of thoughts, she came back to my table and talked some, but not about him. When I asked, she said that he was just a casual friend she knew, who also stayed at Mrs Maher's house and there was nothing more to it than that.

She said that she sometimes came into Ryan's about this time of the evening, and so it was that we met on occasion, when I mostly spent some of my hard earned over the counter. I asked her where she lived now, when she told me that she no longer stayed at Mrs Maher's, but she didn't seem to want to tell me where she lived now and said, "You wouldn't know the place. It's an old caravan at the back of some fields, behind the cemetery."

"Would you show me where it is?"

"Maybe sometime, but not now."

I knew from the way she said it, that her answer was final for the time being.

Then it happened, one evening as I sat in my usual corner, making my pint last, that she had come in, and seemed a bit unsteady on her feet, as she flopped down into the chair opposite.

She looked over at Dave, and soon there was a lot of drink put on the table. Her speech was slurred as she was saying, "Who would have thought it, from all those years ago, that old John Snode would have remembered me."

I asked, somewhat confused, "What about John Snode. Was he not the kind person who helped you in your hour of need?"

"The very same." She was laughing like a fool. Her blouse was unfastened and much of her ampleness was on view.

"Pull yourself together. Do your blouse up. You're drawing looks from the customers, and Dave looks concerned."

For answer, she looked at me strangely as she fumbled with her blouse, but managed after to do more buttons up and said, "Don't you worry about me, my old pal Mal, and get that drink down you. There's more where that came from." Then she added, "Good old John Snode," and raising her glass on high, as if to the heaven, she said, "Saint Peter will look after you, John, for being such a good person to a stray like me."

From what I could gather from her garbled drunken talk, it would appear that Mrs Maher had gone up to The Green where Marie sits at the gates selling her blooms. Mrs Maher told her that John Snode had gone to heaven and that when he was dying, he told her to give the little flower seller £1000 pounds, and she, Mrs Maher, could keep the rest for all her good works on this earth.

It was obvious that Marie was in no fit state to get home on her own, and I looked at Dave for help. Somehow, and I didn't think much about it at the time, Dave seemed to know exactly where the caravan was in the corner of the field, because he said, "Just stay where you are. I'll bring the old jalopy around from the back."

I gathered her basket and finished the drinks, including hers, as she looked through glazed eyes at me from across the table.

Still staring at me, she said, "You are a bit weird, Mal, but I like you in a strange way. If only you'd smarten yourself up."

Dave was at the door beckoning and told his barman to carry on while he was away doing a good turn for a customer.

Outside, the weather was mild for the time of year as I helped her into the back of an old Ford and we chugged off into Grafton Street and up and around The Green. He eventually pulled into a lane at the back of the Mount Jerome Cemetery, and then on to a cart way which led across a field and stopped.

He said to me, "Mal, it's down there," as he pointed to a van parked in the corner among some bushes. "You can manage from here."

"Thank you for your help, Dave. I'm sure when she remembers, she will thank you."

"Don't worry about it. I've got to get back."

He jumped in behind the wheel and was soon out of sight. I helped her, with her head on my shoulders and my free arm around her waist, the other holding the basket. We made slow progress. Marie was out of it and could barely stand.

We were gradually getting closer to the van in among the bushes.

After what seemed an eternity, we got to the door. I put my hand into her commodious coat pocket looking for the key and after rummaging through its various contents, I found it. Happily it worked first turn and I managed to get her up the step and inside, where the bed was down and I let her flop onto it. She was soon snoring away. The van was so untidy, with a small sink full of cups, glasses and various clothes lying around.

I moved some stuff off the easy chair and sat there watching her sleep. In peaceful repose, her once lovely face looked like an angel with no cares in the world.

I thought to remove her coat and shoes and make her more comfortable and started to gently roll her to one side to facilitate my doing so. As I bent over, I was surprised to hear her whisper in my ear, "You are really nice, Mal. You got me home safely."

I was surprised at her fast recovery from the drunk woman of some hours earlier. Then her arms stretched up and pulled me down to her in a very wet-lips embrace. She was now in charge.

She was in command as she went through her menu of everything that a woman can do to make a man happy over and over.

I kept pinching myself to make sure that this was no dream. She was relentless with her lips and full breasts all over my body parts and me so compliant with hers. Nothing was barred when this woman got going. She transported me into places I long remembered from times past. At last we were both totally exhausted and into deep sleep.

I awakened late in the morning from a deep, alcohol-fuelled sleep, to the sound of birds singing in the trees. Quickly realising where I was, I looked around to see she was gone. Her basket was gone and her winter coat. It would appear that her flower-selling came first, no matter what.

I found my clothes and, with a bad hangover, my head full of what had passed the night before, trudged across the field and walked past the graves, back to the road, and I went into Maher's pub for a cure.

After a couple of pints, I was feeling better, and then realised I had arranged to see about my digs.

The next evening I went to Ryan's to look for her, and would you believe she turned up. This time she was sober as a judge. She was smiling as if nothing had happened. She had bought a new dress and looked fresh and as smart as could be.

Dave winked across at me, and he just smiled. It seemed like a scenario which had occurred many times before and it was no big deal.

She obviously had most of the money left, as she was carrying a bag with a Brown and Thomas logo, which was full of clothes.

She came straight to my usual corner table, put the bag down, and waved to Dave, then looking at me said, "Thanks, Mal, for seeing me home safely last evening."

Was that it? Was that all? I couldn't understand it. I was now besotted with this now lovely woman who sold flowers.

"Is that all you've got to say? Didn't it mean anything to you at all?"

Dave was still smiling as he put pints and whisky chasers onto the table.

She pulled a fistful of notes from her pocket and, handing him one, told him to have one on her.

I'm still looking at her, finding it difficult to comprehend, when she said, "Look, Mal, I do appreciate your taking care of me, and Dave of course. I'm sure you were pleased with the way I showed my appreciation. It will happen again. I promise."

It was a promise that would keep me going until I returned from my seasonal stint with the leaves in the parks that we would meet up again. But the one thing I didn't know about was the extent of her friendship with Barney. I was to find out all about that later.

So the end of another season comes and we are paid off until next year. Having declined their invitation to join them in an evening's drinking, our truck driver, Sean, dropped me off at the Green, and not seeing her at the gate with her basket, I made my way down to Ryan's.

The first thing I saw when I opened the door was her and, of course, ******g Barney. Suddenly, the brightness had gone out of the picture. He was half enthusiastic in his welcome. "Hello, Mal, nice to see you back. How are you doing?" All said in a voice full of no concern.

"You haven't been around for months." She seemed to say it in an off-hand manner, as if chiding me for my absence.

"I told you that I would be out in the parks, as usual, tidying up. I told you I'd be away for a bit," I added coldly, in response to her seemingly less than warm greeting.

Barney chimed in, "Yeah, you said you would be going away for a while or so."

I thought to myself, *You'd think I'd been to the North Pole.*

"You're looking nice, Marie." I half mumbled.

I'm thinking to myself, *Where does that prick Barney really fit into the picture?* And I'm hoping she really has a spot in her heart for me. I am so anxious to hope for the possibility that we might continue from that time when she had been warm and accommodating to this frustrated, unfulfilled soul. But I was to learn of Barney's control over her body.

February and March were never my favourite months. They are always cold and slushy. I never seemed to get warm till those months had well passed. The kindly Corporation, who mostly ran the affairs of folk less well off, who lived in our city, would only let me work for them on a seasonal basis, and it used to take me away sometimes for a while. Even on a spring day, I couldn't get warm. It wouldn't be until June that I would really feel warm and my body would sweat a little and I would start to feel some life in tired limbs.

I never had her out of my mind and constantly was trying to guess at what the true story might be about Marie. I sometimes thought of her all day, and sometimes I had the feeling that this woman would not be good for me.

When I asked her about him initially, she looked and told me very unconvincingly, that he was nothing but a very casual acquaintance. I was becoming more convinced than ever that she just regarded me as someone she could use when needed.

She had only told me a part of a story leaving out the bits she knew I wouldn't like. She was not being truthful at all. I recalled incidents of this nature in my life previously. I never felt so frustrated and said, "Now that I'm back from the leaves and the parks, I hope to see you sometimes on your own."

She didn't seem to be too bothered. She just smiled and said, "Sure, Mal, you're always bound to see me here most evenings."

As she is saying this, I'm thinking that I always seemed to be cleaning up after the winter. Tidying up with the other lads. Many with similar backgrounds of those who hadn't passed their exams, but could sweep up the leaves and keep the parks tidy.

We sometimes, when paid, drank more than we should. Perhaps after a long day with the leaves, it was the only consolation in lives with no prospect of anything better. In our various stages of inebriation, there would be some form of card games, mostly a game called 25s, which didn't require too much brain power.

Sometimes there would be females present who would imbibe and, in return, might entertain some of the livelier at the rear of the premises, when darkness and the drink would resolve their biological needs.

Their faces reflected many miles chalked up on the highway of a hard life. Needless to say, these kind, thirsty, lonely, accommodating females would not grace the pages of ladies magazines. Some of our fellows were quite skilled at distilling the same kind of potent fluid that Big J's Father had in the bottle all those years ago. Some of those ladies would drink nothing else, and they never coughed or spluttered. Out in the urban landscape, there would always be some who would have a flask of something quite potent.

In our dress we didn't present a very sartorial picture. We were mostly dressed against the weather in winter waterproofs, dungarees, duffle coats, heavy boots, woollen hats, all Corporation issue. It would be too much trouble for an evening to change that lot, just to go drinking. On occasion, we'd stop to quench a thirst on our way back and leave the truck outside with all the shovels and tools on it, while downing some good cheer and feel the warmth of yet another glass sourced from the soft water of St James Wells.

Some would hold their parts at night. Better than a hot water bottle. Big Dominic had told me he was a confirmed advocate of the relieving habit, which precluded the responsibility of having to please a woman and the expense involved.

Meanwhile, I could not get Marie out of my thoughts. The prospect of perhaps seeing her when I came back had sustained me while I was away. It had given me such a pleasant feeling, although not sure of which way it would go, especially ever mindful of Barney, but there is always hope for fools, is there not? I had been so lonely out there that I didn't want to mix with the other fellows. I was suffering a hunger. I'm always suffering a hunger.

Marie smelled so nice after being exposed to the body odours of those rough but honest fellows. Why does all this race through my mind?

"Well," I said, in a more exasperated tone, "seeing as I'm on my feet I might as well ask what you're drinking."

Barney's face lit up. "Oh, that is very kind of you, Mal. Yeah, I'll have another pint. You were having gin, weren't you, love? Yeah, gin and tonic will do for Marie. You know what she likes."

I thought, I bloody well ought to.

It screwed me up the way he said it with a smirk.

Barman Dave was smiling at the situation. He always seemed a cheerful soul. He was a man who had observed so many scenarios of the human condition.

"'Nice to see you, Mal. All right?"

You'd think I'd been away for ******g years. They surely couldn't know about the other place. I'd kept that quiet. If that ever got out, I'd be so embarrassed.

"I'm fine, Dave. Give them what they want and have one yourself." Dave was such a good sort and had served me many a drink in the past on the slate when I'd been without. He always seemed to want to help where he could. He'd helped me out once or twice during my bad patches and that memorable night when he transported us back to the caravan.

"Thanks, Mal, I don't mind if I do." He pulled himself a half. I gave him the money and as I was taking the drinks over to Marie and Barney I was thinking that I shouldn't have come into the pub. I should have got cleaned up first. I must look a bloody mess with all this outdoor clothing on.

I was remembering again that I had to go round to the old digs and see if Mrs B had kept my room for me. She had once let the room before, because, as she said, "You still owe me rent, Mal." I'd mistakenly thought that this quite elderly senior queen of former times had been compensated in other ways in those winter months.

Had I not been company for her, before I had to go back to the leaves? I did mention it to her, but after some debate, I had agreed upon a certain amount.

Anyway, after getting the money together and paying, she let me back once more and into her favours, but they were favours with love absent.

As I think this, I'm still furious at the casual way Marie had said hello. It made me feel so unwanted. Was I only a convenience for whenever nothing better was on offer?

"Cheers, Mal," Barney's voice grated. "You're very good health."

His concern over my health was something else. It was all so false and very irritating.

I said to Marie, "Is that okay for you?" as I handed her the drink.

"Yes, thanks, Mal," she said with a faint smile.

When I had been with her at first, she'd been so understanding and kind. She hadn't hurried me and it seemed that perhaps she could be me with on a permanent basis. But she never let it happen again. It was as though she just wanted to cope compassionately with the challenge of someone like me. I was more an object of curiosity than of true communion. I'd really thought that at last I'd found someone, even at this late hour.

I was soon to have my thoughts about Barney and her relationship with him confirmed. I now knew that nothing further would ever happen between us. She avoided looking at me as I looked so questioningly at her. I remembered when she had told me that she was keen to find a nice chap who'd give her a better future than Barney seemed to offer. He obviously offered a lot more in those departments where I needed help. Why does that always seem so important? Why did she ever let me know in a kind of a way that she might be available?

Dave was watching. He looked from me to her and read my mind. I kept thinking, *Why should I keep worrying about it?* But I did, and it was doing my attitude to Barney no good at all.

"Good luck," I said as the whisky went down in one go. I don't know why I do that when I'm really stressed.

"Cheers, Mal," they chorused, so it seemed. I thought about my name. What's in a name? Mal, is short for Malachy, short for Mal-function, Mal-fitting, Mal-adroit, Mal-adjusted and mostly Mal-formed. Why do these thoughts flit through my mind when it wants to be full of someone else? What the hell was I doing here now, buying drinks I couldn't afford?

I thought about all those leaves I'd swept up and those parks I'd frozen in. Back to the leaves, millions and millions of them. They'll all be back next year. It's like sweeping up the same old friends again and again. And I'd be doing it all over again with the other sorry souls. What do they call it? Occupational therapy.

My spring will consist of the sap rising, making that which had its winter sleep come alive again and soon to be yet another harvest, as their colour will change, renewing her seasonal cycle and their greeting to me, as all they want to do is say hello again.

I had thought that the clock might turn back for me with her. Could the clock ever turn back for me? Give me just one more moment of bliss, please, my body was pleading. Come on, just one more time. It's always one year older and one year away with the same promise for me, the great executive of the borough park keepers.

Come alive, come alive, it's spring. And in autumn, *Come along again and clear up the mess of your spring. Get your big shovel, your old friends from the trees are waiting.* I looked at Marie as I thought all this. To ever think of how she had made my misshapen body so alive. Even if she cared a little, she could make it all worthwhile and make me come alive again. But I knew deep down it would never happen for me again. I would merely be her curio to be nice to and have around sometimes and maybe a favour from time to time if I kept her glass full. Deep down, knowing the answer was a bitter pill, but didn't I always know the answer, and always hoped I could be wrong? So blindly hopeful is the fool who would cling to a straw.

And then my mind would insist on going on with questions, seeking answers. Why don't you stop crucifying yourself? There must be more to it than that. You have become just another receiver of her favours, as sanctioned by him. Do you want to be with her, under his terms, because that's what it looks like? Is that all you want to be to her? Forget it, or is it worth a desperate last try? Why not? She knows you're not like others. All just because she allowed you access on that never-to-be-forgotten occasion. Had it all been stage managed by her and was I just the puppet, once again? She got to me, because at last, someone seemed to care once again for a brief magical moment that had meant so much.

I knew now, and there was no doubt, that she was completely under his sway and did exactly what he'd allow her to do. She probably told him all about me and how she helped me to manage it again and again. They might even have had a quiet laugh about it.

I could just imagine it, during one of their sessions and with what always ensued afterwards. Providing always that he wasn't too pissed to raise the necessary, after imbibing a massive drop of the grain, of which he was well capable.

As these stupid thoughts were rampaging through my alcohol-fuelled mind and knowing there would be no happy conclusion for this hapless soul, I shouted to Dave, "Dave, I've got a thirst." And I still thought, *What makes me do this so involuntarily?* "I'll have another, Dave. You'll have another, won't you, Marie?" I looked him. "And you Barney?"

Her voice seemed warmer, as she probably was thinking of how much she had got under my skin. She knew that with a flick of her thumb, I was at her beck and call in return for a promise of love in return.

She smiled, as one would indulgently at a pet. "Well, if you insist, Mal. It's very kind of you."

Barney, chipped in, "Thank you, Mal. You're a good sort."

The way I feel, I hardly care what he's saying and think I'd be better off with the other leaf sweepers. They would all be well steamed up by this time and have bought their own drink. They had a strict code about that. I bet Barney has never heard of it, and here I was, getting another drink. Maybe I'm the biggest prick of the lot.

Barney, now preoccupied with his nose and deeply quaffing of my liquid largesse, had gone over to talk to some smart tarty ladies at another table across the room. Maybe I could talk quietly to Marie.

I whispered, "How have you been, Marie?"

"Oh, fine, Mal, fine."

My heart is bursting with hunger, with such a longing to regain my brief magical moment as I mumble, "Didn't you miss me just a little?"

Barney had come back and heard. He smirked, "Of course she missed you, Mal. Didn't you, Marie? You like Mal, don't you Marie?" He said this in a way which told me that she had no secrets from him. I wish he would have a fatal seizure of some kind. He took another large gulp from his glass.

I murmured quietly, "Well, that's me. I'll never change. Maybe it's nice to see the same faces at this time every year."

He was smirking again. "Yes, but last time you said you weren't going back to it. You were making plans, remember?"

He was right. I'd been saying that for the last twenty odd years, and I go back to it every year. I've seen some of the fellows die from various ailments, many of them self-inflicted, through the years to be replaced by others to sweep up the same leaves after each winter. After a while you don't even notice the difference. One day, I suppose, when I can't function any more, they'll give me a caretaker's job where you just sit in a cubby hole of a municipal block all day and brew tea. Ha, that'll be the hat-trick. That'll complete the whole deal. Then cart me away.

"Come on, Mal," Barney was saying. "Where's all that ambition you were talking about?"

That was the last straw. I completely lost it and was expressing my thoughts out loud,

"Why the f*** don't you give it a rest, Barney, and f*** off? What's it got to do with you?" I was surprised at my involuntary outburst. They were all looking at me. The place had gone very quiet.

His only ambition, I thought, was to be a ponce and live off Marie. Dave knows that too. Marie knows it and so did the tarty women he was speaking with earlier. They all knew about him and how he scratched a living off female bodies, including Marie. Everyone had known it except me. The bar was still very quiet.

"Forget it," I said. And myself, I knew I was getting drunk because of a promise, so forget all about that too.

I looked at her in utter desperation, and I didn't care if he heard or not. "Are you going to let him use you to supply his needs like those other ladies at the bar?"

I wondered what she ever saw in him. But I knew the answer to that already. She also needed someone who would manage her previous miserable life and comfort her and, of course, serve a biological purpose, for no fee, when she wasn't serving others, to keep his pot full. I hated him for his use of her body, when to me she would have always been a special queen. With the right man she could have been a lady, even with "a sweeper of leaves." But somehow I knew it was a lost cause. She was never going to leave him.

She whispered, "I'll speak to you later on." It was obvious that she was very aware of the role he made her play, and she was feeling ashamed as it had been made clear to her by my actions.

I knew that my chances were gone, along with the dream that kept me warm last winter.

I could hear me saying, "I'll have another drink, Dave." I looked at her and said nothing and she said nothing as we briefly, without either saying a word, knew it was gone forever as a look passed between us. She made as if to smile in a way which said, "Don't be so upset." It was a pitying look, as she seemed apologetic, like it was with a pang of conscience,

As Dave served my drink, he whispered, "Don't you think you've had enough, Mal?" I nodded mechanically."

Marie said, "Mal, I don't think I ought to have another and I don't want any more."

Why was it important that she have another drink? I don't know. I wonder why I'd got such an urge, and I'm thinking that I would gladly have died for another magical spell with her at that moment.

Why, oh why? Somehow it seems I can't have the woman, but I can have all the booze I want when I have some money. I'd already spent more than I should from my saved seasonal work. I wondered how many leaves I'd have to sweep up for that amount of money. Does it work at a penny a leaf? Maybe if I was really clever I could work it out.

Barney was back with those women at the bar.

Marie repeated firmly, while looking across at those women, with that same ashamed look, "No, don't get me one, Mal."

"All right." My voice betrayed how I felt.

"Now, don't be like that."

"Forget it."

"Look, if it's that important, I'll have another one."

And then in desperation, I whispered in her ear, "Are we ever going to be together? Tell me yes or no, or I'll go mad."

She said sharply, "Be quiet, he'll hear you."

At this time he was busily engaged taking a drink from a middle-aged, big busty woman in a fur coat, saying to her, "That was a generous gentleman I got you the other night."

She simpered, like a fulfilling female on a grand scale and generous as she smiled while passing a large measure of an expensive whiskey across the bar and some legal tender of the right colour. He downed the drink in one gulp, saying, "I'll be seeing you around, Sharon. Next week, I'll have another punter lined up."

Marie was observing all, as she whispered, "Things are difficult at the moment. I'll see you in here same time next week." She continued, in a final cold dismissal as she turned her gaze to the bar and smiled at Barney and Sharon. "That's all I can promise now, and I think you have had enough drink for tonight. You ought to be going."

The queen dismisses her subject, I was thinking, and Barney wasn't taking any notice of us at all. He seemed to be engrossed with Sharon. He carefully put the folding money into his inner pocket.

"All right," I whispered, putting my face close to hers. Maybe what started in March could mean something. And I knew that I was kidding myself.

Barney was now partaking of another drink from the bar and still chatting with Sharon. He raised his glass and smiled across at me. I knew that in his smile he was letting me know he knew everything. Marie looked at him uncomfortably, but smilingly, then quickly looked back to me. She didn't seem to want to talk any more, as if she were afraid of something. Barney was downing his fair share of the Jameson's. I knew he had the whole situation so precisely weighed up. She wouldn't do anything without his consent. He would always have to okay and license any liaison.

Then apparently not to take any notice of my recent little outburst, he smiled again as he walked back to our table. He wiped the excess from his lips as if I'd said nothing and asked, "No offence, Mal. What are you going to do for the summer? Are you going to bum about?"

"What do you mean by that?"

"'Nothing. Nothing all."

"Then don't say bloody stupid things. Maybe I'm not a big success, but I don't sponge on others. Maybe I drink too much sometimes, and although my job is only a seasonal one, it takes enough out of me for the whole year. But I won't be bumming around."

"All right," He said, apologetically. "I didn't mean anything. All right, I'm sorry if I upset you."

"Forget it," I blurted, as I finished my drink. The quicker, the better I thought. The lack of response from her was utterly depressing. I put my empty glass down with a look that said, "I might see you around." She knew I was looking at her in a strange way, and I was feeling bemused and reckless, brought on by the quick intake of alcohol. I didn't care, and for some crazy reason, I started to laugh bitterly while being furious inside. I could see that she was embarrassed.

I just said quietly, "I'll see you then. Cheers." And, looking at him, "You can all f*** off."

Various voices: "See you then, Mal."

"See you, Dave." Marie didn't say anything. She just smiled and looked at me benignly, as I was going out the door. I could still hear the laughter and Dave's voice as I was going out, "See you, Mal."

It was raining hard outside and I was burning up inside. I could only think about her and how ridiculous and pathetic I must seem. No way would she even think seriously about me now. And to think, she was mine for that brief moment. Or was she ever? She'd still got some good looks, but she'll go downhill if she stays with that ponce, with the moth-eaten pullover and the oily hair, for that's what he was, when you added it all up. She didn't really make a living from the flowers alone, and I had to accept the fact that she earned her money in other ways to keep his appetites fed, fuelling his body with drink and everything else he desired.

Surely, she prefers to be a sometimes lady of the night to an honest fool like me, who would have been her slave if she had really cared.

Of course, I knew that I'd never be as slick as he was. He probably looks better in his old polo neck than I do with my best suit on ... if I had one. I never was one for clothes much. The fashion men don't make them with the misshapen in mind.

I pulled the hood of my duffle over my head as I trudged through the rain. For some strange reason, I cast my mind back to Eamonn, my younger brother, on those rainy cold winters when we used to walk to school and listen to his continual cough. The last thing he ever said to me on this earth was, "Mal, do you remember when Ma bought us those suits with the money from St Vincent de Paul and we looked so nice when we made our First Holy Communion. Didn't we look great?"

Those were the last words he ever said. My mother had just kept looking out of the window, with her handkerchief to her face. "Did you hear what he said?" I had shouted at her. "Did you hear what he said? He's gone from us and it's your fault."

How could I say a thing like that as his eyes closed? She'd turned her face to me, which was full of tears. She held me close as we both cried. The nurse said nothing and pulled the sheet over dear Eamonn's face, now in saintly repose.

Oh hell, why am I thinking about this now? It was such a long time ago and now my mind is riveted back to where I am. She, who I wanted so badly, was still in there with that awful pr***.

On the way back to my friendly landlady, Mrs McBhann, I thought to stop and have another at Slattery's. When I opened the door I saw Ted.

"Hello, Mal. You're back, then?"

Ted was such a kindly man, who seemed to understand everybody. I could always have a quiet drink with him. We'd killed one or two, on occasion. I felt he could identify with me, and made me feel so much at my ease.

He continued while studying me with a smile, "Mal, you could use a shave couldn't you?" Then he added good-humouredly, "And I can tell, that you've had a few? This is your time of the year, eh? Finished now, until next year?"

I echoed, "Until next year, Ted."

"Oh, by the way, there was a big lady came in here looking for you a few days back."

I said laughing, a bit cynically, "You're joking. Who would be looking for me, eh?"

"I'm not kidding, Mal. You know the one. When you were in here last year, you were both a bit steamed up, remember?" And still looking at my querying gaze, he continued, "You know the one from the boarding house. Anyway, she said if you came in to tell you that your room was there if you wanted."

"Oh, you're talking about Mrs McBhann. Why didn't you say? That was all settled when I paid her up to date. I'd better take one along for old time's sake."

Ted always seemed to remember what everybody liked. He smiled knowingly. But I didn't mind. As I was thinking this, I thought that even Mrs B, the old queen, the old reliable, she even had her price. Another lonely soul and her little comforts supplied by such as me and others of similar frugal means, but with nature's oldest needs. I suppose there were worse things to endure than having to spend the cold winter nights backing up to her ample rear. We kind of mutually understood that she was my very last safety net. No doubt, in her past, she had been a queen to someone. The old saying, like, "Any port in a storm," could describe Mrs B.

Meanwhile my mind was furiously thinking about Marie and Barney. It seemed that I couldn't get them out of my mind. Why was I so mad? Did it reflect every failure at this stage in my life? It was all boiling up inside me.

Caravan Fury

It got so bad that all I could think about was what mischief to be doing. It had come to a fine pass, now that I couldn't even hold on to a slow runner. I knew I was moving inexorably into that later phase of my existence when time is fast running out, and the thought made me even more frustrated and that made me more furious.

Even Ted's consoling words didn't help, as I got more under the influence of the drink and tried to think of some way to do something terrible to Barney, who had dismissed me as more or less as an oddity when I couldn't rid myself of the thought that he had allowed me to have the use of her services, i.e. "a nice time with his chattel."

I firmly believed he had allowed it, just to keep the pot boiling and his pint pot filled by those ladies, and even this craving fool who was so desperate in his quest for a last possible queen.

The whole episode consumed me all the more, as I thought about how I had, in all reality, been dismissed. No doubt, and I repeat, that he had been very amused when she'd recounted the details to him, and they had their laugh about my most personal moments with her.

It's amazing how I thought all this in the fraction of a moment as the drink fuelled my hate and it filtered through this addled brain, which can function at breath-taking speed in unproductive areas. It was the same brain which found so much difficulty, when confronted with their simple puzzles and blocks, when tested under their "white coated" rules.

Ted's voice broke through the haze, breaking into my rampant brainstorm, "Come on, Mal, it's time to go. You've had plenty. Why do you keep mumbling to yourself?"

My speech must have been very slurred, as I tried to say something. I just nodded at him with a sheepish grin.

"Don't forget Mrs B's little bit of sustenance." He stuck the peace offering into my duffle pocket as I almost stumbled through the door into the road.

"Goodnight, Ted, and thanks. You're a good man." The words were so slurred that I don't think he understood what I was mumbling.

As I went into the cold night, I just wanted to walk for miles to try and clear my head. I couldn't get these two out of my thoughts. I decided to take the lane which cut through the cemetery. I remembered where the field was at the other side, where her caravan was.

I was headed by instinct in that direction. I must have walked for ages. As I walked, and half stumbled, I kept sipping from Mrs B's bottle, which wasn't really mine and should have been enjoyed with Mrs B as in the past. I felt I was stealing her drink, but that just made it all the more wicked and I wanted to be wicked.

I seemed to be dropping into a haze, as my body became more overpowered with the alcohol. The hour was now quite late and I felt so tired. I stumbled through the graveyard, among the head-stoned beds, of those in a permanent state of rest, of which many, no doubt, had been down my path in their time. They could have told me that there was nothing new to suffer or to tell.

As I made my unsteady footsteps among their defined cots, I stumbled again and struck my head against the sharp corner of a marble headstone. The impact dazed me, and I subsided into a sitting position on the slab of a resident who wouldn't mind, I thought, and soon my head lay down to share their space, and I fell into deep sleep. I must have been comatose for some time.

Was my stupor really disturbed by the tapping of chisel on granite? As I shook myself, it scared the **** out of me, for the spiritual-ness of the next world was still deeply engrained from childhood under the strictures of those who shape our "other promised world" of spiritual happiness forever.

Then I espied the cause of the noise, or did I imagine it? Did I see a very old man sitting astride the grave next to me, with hammer and chisel, clad only in a white shroud and a snow white beard hanging down past his waist? He was chipping away at the marble lettering on the headstone.

"What the **** do you think you're doing? You nearly scared the shite out of me. What the **** are you doing?"

A very old voice said, "It's not my fault if they spelt my name wrong, is it?"

I blinked and when I looked again, there was no one there, but sure enough there was an old chisel and hammer lying on the marble plinth. I felt some wet on my forehead when I touched it, and could see the blood from my collision with the headstone some hours earlier.

As I came fully back to my senses, my mind riveted back to him and her. I raged inwardly as I thought that he would be well on his way with their cavorting antics by now. That sod could drink such a lot and still stay on his feet, when others would be falling about and no doubt still do what was expected of him when she would lay down to do his bidding. I couldn't stop thinking that now they would be nice and snug in that old ramshackle caravan of his. It would still be in the corner of Dolan's field, overlooking the gravel dirt road below, from the time they had been taking gravel from the quarry, so long ago, that it was now blending with the landscape and all the growth which had since, more or less, covered the diggings of the past.

I now accepted the fact that he had allowed her to be with me, and had made himself conveniently absent.

I remember telling her with tears and longing that I was besotted. She had just smiled when I surfaced from among her thighs remembering how I had kissed and caressed my first ever queen, and she giggled like a schoolgirl as she sucked my privates so vigorously.

It was the kind, caring way she had truly accommodated me. It did occur to me then that she was a most experienced practitioner, in all departments, in making men happy and satisfied with such clients that Barney would supply from time to time.

It had also occurred to me since, that the bent c*** could have been looking at us through the window. Oh no, that really would be the end, and I was getting too fanciful. But the more I thought about it, the more I now became obsessed with the thought that he could have been peeping at us. The thought made me walk faster and take more solace from the bottle.

Why not? Mrs B. wouldn't mind me going for broke and finishing off her peace offering. I found myself walking quicker and my steps leading me in the direction of the field where the caravan was parked.

It seemed I had been walking forever when I could now make out the dim light in the distance. I walked through the gap in the hedge and remembered all those years ago when I'd watched the girls and felt childlike and sneaky, and I approached nearer and nearer.

In the very late hour the light glowed dimly from within the old van. I could faintly hear jig music wafting through the window and thought that maybe he was keeping the beat in his oscillatory movements.

I was now up close against the side of the caravan. I raised my eyes very gradually and peeped through a slit in the dirty well-faded curtains. There they were in full flow with him atop, bottle in hand, and delivering therapy, seemingly keeping time to the up-beat jig music. Marie was naked as the day she was born, moving and moaning in a joyous agony of fulfilment, which told me all that I knew already—my heavenly interlude could only have been a passing fancy with a weird new toy for her amusement. But the main feature would always be Big Barney, who knew about the kind of pills to take for even more added stimuli.

My most burning thought as I watched was, *How can I undo him? How can I cause him some terrible grief?* Even as I thought it, I started to gather dry branches from the nearby woods. The blood still trickled down from the gash in my forehead, inflicted by my difference with the gravestone. The alcohol was numbing the pain. I was literally racing around in the industry of preparing for his ultimate demise.

I soon had a pile of small dry twigs under the caravan. I pulled the old newspaper from my pocket and managed to get a fire going with the aid of my old petrol lighter. The rain had stopped some hours ago and, with the help of a soft breeze, the flames were fast gathering momentum. I put a strong branch against the handle of the outward opening door and watched the now blazing fire as I crazily looked at them cavorting while the very flames were licking the worn dry paintwork on the side of the van.

"Go on! Keep going you f*******, keep going," I half shouted at them through the window as the heat was growing in intensity. Soon they would be in the raging inferno. Hell on this earth would be visited upon the ponce Barney for the wrongs and sins he'd committed. And what of my feelings for her? Would all be made pure in the final cremation of her much miss-used body in the cleansing flames?

The fire was now enveloping the van, and I was getting burned as I watched fascinated while they blissfully continued their ecstatic writhing. Then the heat must have at last started to impinge, as he stopped and jumped up from her with his huge erection wobbling. As he moved so quickly, it subsided fast. He started to shout as the glass cracked in the heat, the flames bursting in amid the shattering breaking glass. Then he saw my burnt, drunken, bloodied face flattened against the side window.

He leaped in the air and, in a reflex action, when he couldn't open the door, ignoring her, dived though the end panoramic window, out and through the hedge and straight down onto the hard, gravel road below. He was moaning like someone in agony and trying to move. His self-saving act had been one of self-preservation, leaving her to her impending doom.

Mad as I was, I couldn't see her suffer and, pulling my duffle over my face, I pulled the branch away and crashed my way in through the door. Enveloping her in the duffle, I dragged her naked body though the now shattered, heat-searing gap and threw her down beside me in a heap on the grass.

She screamed and shouted and there was my blood from the wound dropping on to her white flesh. It seemed to be everywhere.

She was screaming, "You're mad, you're mad!" She kept screaming.

"Why did you do it? What have I ever done to you? I took pity on you. That's all the thanks I get for trying to be nice to you, you horrible little ****! You stupid eejit!"

Now she was scrambling in all her nakedness down to the road and crying over him and he was still moaning in pain, obviously having injured himself as he jumped, severely cutting himself in the groin area. There was blood all over. It was like an impromptu circumcising of sorts, I thought, as my warped mind raced.

I clambered down and put my coat over her as she shivered beside her real suffering master. I couldn't help thinking, as the caravan burned with such ferocity, that just a moment ago their world was complete, and for the first time I was glad that others had to suffer. Barney was shaking so violently that I felt a bit sorry for him for that brief moment.

The fire brigade sirens could be heard as they approached. Obviously someone had seen the flames and dialled the fire services. In through the gate they took their hoses and worked to put the flames under control. When they finished, there was nothing much except a pile of smouldering, steamy ashes—all that was left of a place that had seen so much pleasure for some. The ambulance men arrived. We were taken to the hospital. Later, many questions and serious charges were made against me.

Incarceration

Eventually when my history and papers were brought to bear, I was once more incarcerated where I could be under their secure care. The burnt facial skin, which has left its searing scar, as well as the granite headstone, all tell their tale.

Barney had to have extensive surgery carried out to save those parts of his body.

The injuries caused by his plunge through the window of the dilapidated caravan will always be a reminder of a sinful life and its price indelibly printed. Marie still had most of the money left by John Snode, and by all accounts, found a new life in England.

Meanwhile, for me, in my place of correction, I met others who had their own various mental proclivities. All with their story to tell. There was one in particular, who would sit next to me in those periods when the inmates were allowed to socialise, so to speak, and be allowed to walk within the confines of the highly walled grounds. I liked just to sit on my own in a secluded spot and watch the activities of others, who would kick a ball or engage in other physical activities, some with each other among the shielding bushes and trees. Old habits die hard. Mostly the others didn't bother with me. There was no doubt that some regarded me as a way-out oddity, a one off, as I would sit and ruminate on nothing and everything in general, drifting back to sitting close on a horse with Sarah, of heavenly queens, and of burning caravans pulling naked Marie through the flames, wafting through a mind so full of yesterdays. Even Steph the Leg and her magic lips would remind this social miscast of happy relieving moments when craving needs were fulfilled among the trees. Only when alone did I feel comfortable, dwelling on my most private thoughts. Among the guests of our corrective environment was this unshaved man, who had let his greyish beard grow over most of his face. He would sit on the end of the long seat and say nothing while gazing into nowhere in particular and always, for whatever reason, keep his hands dug deep in the pockets of an old greasy raincoat, no matter what the weather. He would sit for ages and say nothing, but would turn and stare at me, which I espied him doing from time to time. One day, eventually, he spoke to me. I didn't answer at first, but when he said to me in a soft shy nervous voice, "I know about you, Mal. I know you have had problems, and I can tell you that it's not always our fault, because that's what the psychiatrist told me."

I had to ask him. "What have you been told by the men trained to read and fix our minds?"

Seaneen, for that was his name, told me that the Garda had pulled him in lots of times, because he kept opening his rain coat when up in the park and showing passing ladies what nature had blessed him with. The highly qualified and much learned psycho man who read his mind after many sessions, told him that it was a compulsion, because he was so shy. He couldn't talk to women and tell them what was on his mind because of a chronic mental block, which was the cause of such shyness. The seeds had been sown many years ago, when he was so young, as a result of very severe admonitions by the pastors when, in confession, he told them that he enjoyed playing with himself, resulting in such strictures of the enormity of his crime and the prospect of a life in burning flames in the hereafter if he didn't desist, that it had shaped a mind and forever blocked any normal form of communication with the opposite sex. The only way left to him was to flash his outstanding nature, by way of salutation, like saying hello.

It was compulsive. He told me that, "I just could not stop doing it." When I asked him if he would ever be cured? He said to me, very earnestly, "When they let me out of here, they know that in a short while I will be back yet again for more corrective treatment and mind readings." Then he added, "But I've made up my mind,

I am definitely going to try and stop doing it. I am definitely going to give it up. I've really made up my mind this time to stop doing it." And then, as an afterthought, he added, with a serious face, "But perhaps, I'll just stick it out until the cold weather really starts."

More years have passed and they have come to tell me, "You'll have to get ready to go out today. He's gone and they want you to be there with the mother when saying a last goodbye."

Two keepers dressed me in a suit. I was sad and frightened by it all, and depressed even more than usual. And Mother, so old now, looked at me through tears and said, "Mal, he never really knew you. You were always such a great worry to him."

For the most stupid of reasons all I could think of was the day that the gun dog took off. I said, "Do you remember the dog?" I was crying as I spoke. She looked at me tolerantly as one would an uncomprehending child.

People stood around the grave as the soil was shovelled onto the varnish. I always wondered why they bothered to paint the box—it's all going to fall apart after a while. Mother kept staring at it, as it slowly vanished from view under the clay. She was looking at it in a way that seemed to suggest he might shove the lid off and rise up, get out, and say, "It's all a mistake. I've changed my mind. I'm perfectly well. Let's go home."

Mother turned and was now looking hard at a younger woman standing some way off with a veil over her face. She had a hankie to her eyes. For one brief spell she had been his young queen all those years ago, when he had left our home for her, until stern advice from her pastors had prevailed, and on the basis of such powerful influences, he had been discarded and had returned to our *ménage* where he had been forgiven.

The voice of the Holy Pastor droned through the ritual as he wondered if his next client for the promised world would be on time. He had a tight schedule. His holy words wafted through my brain, Nomine, Patri . . .

Mid-winter is a busy time when the flu and bronchitis and even malnutrition take their toll in a green land of plenty, but not for some. There's always a busy season in any business, and like any other, the death business is no different. I looked at her, so frail now. How could she ever have been so big and magnificent and so beautiful? She, who had been my earliest memory of a fleshy mountain to climb. Was it an infant's mind that magnified it for all time?

And now that he's gone, would I once again be considered as a substitute? Would she have more time for me now? No, perhaps not, there's too much time gone, too much space, too many hurts and a yawning void with no time left. Impossible.

The Reverend Father's voice had stopped after he splashed holy water over the grave. He was talking to her now and then coming over to me. He looked at me curiously. This now so very old holy man, well close to his century, remembered me well. He knew that time will never erode all the defects, and consignment will be the true determiner in due course. He, who wore His collar, was secure in a belief that he would always be His faithful servant, doing His work until called to Him. He laid a hand on my shoulder and I received his blessing, as he said, "God be with you always, dear Mal. Never forget, we're all His children."

She cried as she wrapped the blanket round my legs before they wheeled me away.

Then it was business as usual. I go back to the little room with the bars and the blocks and the puzzles and a chamber pot full of daydreams and the kindly keepers in their white coats. I was crying. I don't know why, I really don't. It's not because I was feeling sorry over him. I was crying over me, as I feel I'm in isolation and detached from it all, and crying just came naturally.

Not since my illness, when I didn't want to ever go out again, did he ever come to see me. And he in the same house where I could hear his voice just a few seconds away downstairs. I must have been a terrible disappointment to him. But could I help it? He could never understand my dread of just going out there among them, to be failed yet another time. I couldn't take it.

Deep down, inwardly, I never forgave him for letting dear old Cecil carry on working his heart out, when he hired him out for a few paltry shillings a day and no vet at hand in his hour of need. I would have nursed him for the rest of his life. It had broken my heart. Couldn't he have just understood as a father? He could never understand that I needed him more in the later years. At least her sometimes mechanical "And how are you today?" through the years had been some form of contact and comfort for your issue crying in the void.

And now it seems I'm taking longer and longer spells at rest. No more get up and go.

So much time.

Why bother? They've taken care of everything. I'm not even allowed my dreams any more. That last one was so long ago. Then they came to see me, and I didn't want to see them. I told them I didn't want to talk. I just wanted time to think, and she of the large back is now so vague in a memory that does not want to remember. The last time she came to see me, she was wheeled in her own wheelchair. Did she remember, I wondered, as I looked at her old face, that it was she who had slapped me over four score years ago? She had been so beautiful. It's funny that I should think of that as I look into her wrinkles. Her words of comfort sometimes had an unsettling effect because they were too late, too late. Jesus Christ, I wanted them a lifetime ago. Now I lie here, waiting for the boneyard. Someone wheeled me back to my dream cell. And he who sired me is gone forever, who never heard my silent craving cry, although only a whisper away.

Epilogue

Is it possible to meet someone just once and never forget her and to love and adore her for the rest of your life? When I wanted to go and see her they said I couldn't go. It was to be my last attempt. Mind you, I knew they wouldn't have it. They wouldn't wear it, not since that last little episode. It wasn't my fault. It was all because of meeting Dave. Dave, Dave, I can't take it anymore. You let me get as pissed as a fart and the police car brought me back. The Doc thought it was funny. None of the others did. He'd just commented, "You're too old now, old timer, for that sort of thing. You've got to take it easy."

Too old? Never too old to see dear Mrs B, who kept me warm just like the old queen she truly was with her ample rear that had warmed many a needy soul, always available to provide a loving release to those in need of a little warmth in their dreary lonely lives. They said she came in one day, but I was fast asleep and they didn't want to wake me. After watching me for some time, she left a bottle of Jameson and hurried away.

What's age when there's a queen to command? You'd think I'd been here a hundred years by the way they go on. It was all just because I made a mess. They shouldn't blame me for that. I told them I was quite capable of going on my own, but Big Sister Bum Farrell, that's what I call her, said, "No way, old soldier."

Of course she had to say that. She said, "From now on, we're going to treat you like a baby. That way," she continued, "we're not going to have any more accidents or trouble with you or your natural functions, are we?"

She was imperious as she said that, and that was final. She told them I had done something very naughty when she was putting me in my chair. All bloody lies, all lies.

Like the day when she was talking to Matron and had her back to my bed, sort of half-sitting on it, and I, in peak, for I didn't like that mass sitting on my bed, had dug my nails in under her bottom. She never even let on that she'd noticed. She just moved away, ever so casually, and gave me a withering look. And she smiled like you'd hardly notice, as if to say, "I'll get even with you another time." I secretly admired her queenliness for that.

And when I missed the urine bottle, and wetted the floor, she strode in and gave me one of her withering looks. I mumbled, "Sorry, but you didn't bring it to me in time." She just lifted me out of the bed as if I were a feather.

She was so strong, I thought. She took everything off the bed. Now onto the wheelchair, now down to the big bath. The water was too warm. Two of them, now, and they don't care, as they giggled and were laughing at each other and looking at me.

One said to the other, "This game old beggar will never go. Come on, Granddad, up this end. Isn't that better?"

And they laughed like mad when I said, "Who's getting in with me for a giggle?"

They just laughed at me.

Isn't it marvellous when you're so old and drugged? Then it's funny and they don't care what I say.

Then she came in, the last of the big queens, Big Sister Bum. "How is our elderly gentleman behaving?"

And they both replied, as with one voice, "He's fine, Sister."

"Have you washed his hair?" And so saying, she filled the cup from the cold tap, doused my head, and made me start and shiver, saying the while, "Have a cup of good cheer for bottom gropers."

Ooh, I thought, *you remembered that, didn't you? Oh, ten out of ten to you.* I had to admire the Bum. What a queen she'd have made. She'd have been majestic. I looked at her and said, "I'm sorry about what I did the other day."

"So am I, Pops." Then she gave me the quickest kiss on the forehead, saying to the other two,

"Get him wrapped up nice and warm, we don't want him to catch his death. His bed is made and I've put a hot bottle in it." She smiled briefly at me.

And with the one voice, the two said, "Yes, Sister."

I knew that she must have been a true queen to someone at some stage. I remembered the time when I stayed in the toilet and they had to break the bolt to get it open. I guess she had her reasons for doing what she did that last day when I'd definitely made up my mind to go and see my last old queen, Mrs B. How could they stop me? How could they be so unkind?

I might not feel like it tomorrow, or never again. I feel so tired and sleepy. All those queens, they seem so far away now, in a haze. Everything is in a haze, so hazy.

Where is she? Where is she? I might as well ask if she came. Why bother? You know somehow she'll come, she's got to. She said she would. I know she'll come. That look and knowing that look sometimes perhaps in the misshapenness of the one you bore.

Had I been handsome, she probably would have been more sympathetic to my plight and brought to tears. It was the oddity of me that had appealed. And how can I believe in the weirdness of the facts? Not borne out by any of the acts, but she'll come, I know it, otherwise what would be the point of it all? She is now at the century mark.

Could I ever recapture a moment of the milk-white, milk-whiteness, of her motherly-ness and closeness? She had been made a mother when still in her teens. Could I have possibly been so near to touch those lips with my lips? Oh, teacher, teacher, where are you? Just let me lick and caress you once again.

They are just patterns, especially about someone who will remain forever indelibly printed. But why go on and think about her any more. And stop worrying, she'll come. Come on, forward to your dream. Forward. Stop. Start.

You could never be happy, except when and within their rules indelibly inscribed. And was I ever the principal actor in this piece? Is it the real piece? Did I act with her, my loved one, in such rawness? Was I the king fitted for the queen when she lay there? Was I just paying homage? In that world, the world of needing someone, being fulfilled in the dark room, in our restless quest to arrive. My journeying will never be complete. And why not be left in peace to remain, but she must come.

They were the smiling faces, who could never understand it. What have I got to smile about? Well, they're the fools and I'm the clever one. Look at them, all at their great pace, seeking, striving. *To what end?* I ask myself. Racing in their white coats, hither and tither, to get to the top of somewhere in their lives, as they would purportedly help us. To what end?

Sometimes I can tell it's going to be a bad day. Nothing will make me move on such a day. They can shout all they want to, but I am secure in my cot. Why listen to the utter banality of what they have to say? It doesn't matter what they say when the whole framework of my body is alight, physical and mental. They are my days. They're my days for staying still. They're milestones that form part of the journey through the void, whether you be at spring, summer, autumn, and even now for me so cold, so cold in my winter. I'm always cold now and it seems to be always winter.

"Where's my hot drink? Where are my tablets?"

I remember she said to me all that time ago, "Don't try to find out what I'm thinking. Wait till I'm asleep and ask me what I am dreaming, and you'll know me better."

She was right. She was always right in so many things. Didn't she know me so well? Why was I so unkind when you stretched across to kiss me? Was I the last straw? Was I the last vestige of close connection, and you now so small and shrunken? Could I have possibly gazed at your great whiteness and felt so lonely? So utterly lonely? I would never forgive you for the isolation which drove me into my own prison where my dream was the only key to ease a caged mind, which was stronger than steel bars, for all time held inextricably.

Next Wednesday you said you'd be back. It was always a Wednesday that was your day for the weekly contact with your imperfect one.

I laughed hysterically the last time, remember? I shouted that one Wednesday you wouldn't come. I wanted it, and yet I dreaded it. I hated the thought, but I knew one Wednesday, with all those years on your face that you just weren't going to come. And I knew it must be soon now. Would I be free? Free of all connection? Stupidly free, just free from the one person who ever really cared. To be free from the true mother queen? Then it happened.

She who had been our great soup maker and housecleaner and washing machine, who used to stand at the sink for hours on end and a father who wouldn't even put a coin in her slot of love, the slot of life itself. That's all she needed to keep going. He never even thought about it. All boilers need to be stoked. No other maintenance needed.

The nurse and the doctor came in to tell me. The doctor and Nurse Big B, the only friends I have here, never forgetting the doc with his magic loaded needle, for switching me off.

I can still remember her handsome white face with snowy white hair, sitting in the wheelchair. The doc told me that she wouldn't be coming anymore. He looked so sad and sorry for me. I remember him saying, so gently, "Mal, she won't be wheeled in anymore. She has gone at last to rest from this life's labours."

I mumbled, "It's alright, Doc, I knew it had to be sometime." The washing machine is now R.I.P. Amen. They'll never recycle that unique piece of loving machinery. Never were clothes so white. And when she lay there, so still, she looked so queenly in tranquil repose. At last, a saintly lifeline gone forever.

So I can lie here and think about it, but my cup is emptying fast. Why can I be so matter of fact about it? Why go through the emotion and experience of it all? Why rehash it every time you're feeling a bit sorry for yourself? I had often wondered if she'd just make the century, and she did. Did she ever really love me with other than a motherly love? Why the hell am I blabbing all over? "No, Doc, no. Don't, don't switch me off. I'm all right. Just let me suffer for a while. Leave it. I'll be alright, honestly."

"Very well, let me know if there's anything you want, Mal."

I was clinging to his hand a little as I whispered, "Thank you, Doc."

I knew he was only trying to ease the pain.

The suffering we live with in the hope that joy will come of it as a reward for our pain is written so deeply in the belief that things will get better to assuage simple minds.

My homeward inward journey would commence, bringing a feeling of absolute relief, which was welling up inside me. I struggled to get back into the vortex, back into her.

Back to where I came from, the re-channelling, the re-cycling, the re-fabrication of all my used up tissue, and I know that I'll have no peace until I'm safe inside her once more. Oh mother of the entire universe, why didn't you wait for me? In the way we knew so much of our life threads which grew so brittle in old age. Why did you leave before me? Wait and wait? Your child is crying. The only cure for my ailment is you.

Every thought I had was hers. It was all so innocent, so innocent. Even in our forbidden moments when we had found each other, there was always the human element and the guilt, which robbed us of the dream that should have been so beautiful and pure. And the deed perpetrated, holy and unholy, was beyond the physical. To have loved and to have done what we did, such imagery, even in the nightmares, the frightening ones, leaves a lesson to be learned and teaches us that we must never have the very thing for which we crave, as I remembered a loving family on a beach so long ago.

Why do we remember all so well, when time is running out, and retrace the tiniest moment from the way I played it when it was my turn. I'm slipping into the final days of depression, in the realisation of a pup's foolishness.

Turn the clock, back, back, oh so far back as I look at "our" photograph still fading on an old paper patterned wall.

A picture so softly faded
The vogue then, To be shown in sepia
As soft shaded, we sat there,
In front of his lens
Dilating an iris, To let the light in,
As you held my hand,
Although no light Would ever shine there,
Only head and shoulders,
And the wax flowers.
I remember your new dress
And thought, what a shame
That it wouldn't be shown
In the patterned frame.
He knew our loving hands
Would be pictured not,
And he smiled like a man
Who'd seen such a lot . . .?
. . . as yet uncoupled,
Before his Fox Talbot box
As he touched the magnesium
To light loves young dream?
We sat there
Just us, and the whole world,
Inside our new clothes
Two hearts so full
Of hope, of love,
In our likeness together
I'm looking at sepia paper
And the image of flesh is fading
In the caress of time
To a weeping whiteness
Oh Jesus, It's too late to cry now.

Should I have known me better? I who have learned so much, can do nothing to extend my lease, due to expire.

All those years have gone. I should have gone to see her, but that was yesterday and the day before, before, and before, because you knew deep down, that you just couldn't take it, if she said, "Go away."

Explore the darkest roots when assessing the debits and credits. Just blank out all previous experience, so that one's reaction is not conditioned by anything in the past. Impossible? We are cursed by a memory which is rarely neutral? What would happen to all our yesterdays if we didn't continually regurgitate our most memorable moments.

And so I think of you. Your touch was for the first time and will always be new. It had no reference point. You confounded every previous experience and left your indelible mark on me forever, and in that miracle of love, you gave this misshapen soul such warmth, which only a mother could give without exaction or price and a promised immortality which would cheat life itself.

In my body, guided by the unknown, outside of my mind and nothing physical interfering, transportation is complete. No more will there be a price to pay. Everything will be beautiful and no-one will be hurt again as I go into my final dream, speeding through the clouds on my dear old Cecil, who has come to take me home. I know we won't ever stop again, as we move as one at the speed of light.

Looking into ourselves
At the person who dwells
The observer with the prying eye
Objectivity, to be the aim
In the final analysis game
Softly whispered,
In a last good bye.

Endgame

Nurse Big B was shouting, "Doctor, Doctor, I think he's gone. Seems strange, it must have been those drugs you had him on. They seem to have stimulated his mental processes towards the end. He just kept talking about bicycles and queens and someone named Cecil, and his Mother. It was sometimes like he was awake. His eyes would open and he'd talk and talk as if he was speaking to someone in the room. Then he seemed to go so quickly."

Not seeming to notice or hear her last remark, the Doctor murmured, as if talking to himself, "Yes, sometimes that drug has some very odd effects."

He remembered one case where the patient had experienced being born, and even described to him the discomfort of coming through the birth canal.

Nurse Farrell nodded, with a tear in her eye, "It was a bit weird, when I would sit here and listen to him. He would recall the most quirky things with women which had happened to him in his traumatic life. Sometimes I would be fascinated by his ramblings as if the other person was here with him. And, Doctor, it was only weeks ago that we had that incident with me?"

The doctor restrained a smile. "Yes, I remember."

He recalled Mal telling him that he would have one more queen before he'd go and it had to be Big Nurse Bum. The Doc had just smiled at the time, having got used to his ramblings. Then the incident had occurred.

She was so embarrassed when she related what had occurred. Apparently, he'd called her over to fix the bed. He'd complained that his pyjama cord was too tight and he had asked her to put her hand under to undo the cord and loosen it. He seemed so helpless. While she was undoing the knot, he suddenly grabbed her hands and clasped them around his parts. She was so surprised at his strength that she couldn't move her hands before he had convulsed and made such a mess into them.

She had run out of his room shouting, "That dreadful little devil, you wouldn't believe what he has done." She ran to the basin and washed her hands furiously.

The doctor smiled again at her repeating the event as he lifted the inert wrist and pulled the sheet over a face which was at last in peaceful repose.